ZK

The Girl
Who Slipped
Through Time

Also by Paula Hendrich

Who Says So?

The Girl Who Slipped Through Time

Paula Hendrich

Lothrop, Lee & Shepard Company
A *division of William Morrow & Co., Inc.*
NEW YORK

Copyright © 1978 by Paula Hendrich
All rights reserved. No part of this book may be reproduced or utilized
in any form or by any means, electronic or mechanical, including
photocopying, recording or by any information storage and retrieval
system, without permission in writing from the Publisher. Inquiries
should be addressed to Lothrop, Lee & Shepard Company, 105 Madi-
son Ave., New York, N. Y. 10016.

Printed in the United States of America.

First Edition
1   2   3   4   5   6   7   8   9   10

Library of Congress Cataloging in Publication Data

Hendrich, Paula.
    The girl who slipped through time.

    SUMMARY: A time warp takes a girl from the 21st century to
Kansas in the 1930's where she joins in a feud with ecological im-
plications for her own time.
    [1. Space and time—Fiction.   2. Conservation of natural resources—
Fiction]   I. Title.
PZ7.H3854Gi   [Fic]   77-17947
ISBN 0-688-41836-8
ISBN 0-688-51836-2 lib. bdg.

To Suzanne and Melissa

1

I don't expect you to believe what I am about to say. There is no way I can verify it scientifically. I can only say that it is absolutely true. If my parents weren't so strongly pair bonded, Father might have been more aware of what was happening that day it all began. Mother had just called him on our tele-com, and they were so absorbed with each other that he didn't notice I had slipped away. He knew I was angry and upset, but he didn't care! At least that was how I felt about it then.

Not that I had started out feeling angry and up-set, not at all. It was a special favor to be given a chance to go on that expedition with Father. Oh,

I'd had a few moments of doubt about it—students at the Collegium who get special privileges can become suddenly unpopular. But I didn't care about that, not really. Father had asked for me. For me! As far as I knew, it was the only time in all my fourteen years that he'd ever asked for special favor for me.

To say I was excited can't express my feelings. In the fourth decade of the twenty-first century, few people ever see the part of the country where we were going. And we were going alone! Mother couldn't get away from her work just then, and I would have Father's full attention the whole time. At least that's what I thought—and I suppose that's what made this trip so special to me.

Of course, mere physical distance couldn't separate my parents. They are together even when they're apart. I know that, and sometimes it's hard being the child of parents as totally committed as mine—I mean to each other, as well as to their work.

It is a rare thing, this pair bonding. Most of my schoolmates had seen a succession of matings and couplings and platonisms in their parents' relationships. They accepted parental affection, or the lack of it, very casually. I was different. Not because my father is Dr. Jason Picard and my mother Dr. Athena Foster; certainly not just because they had become famous as the eco-research team who had planned the colonization of Terra Two before that project was dropped. No, I was different because—well, because I had this need to be a part of them. I longed

8

for a sense of—what is that archaic word? Family. They were my family, so why did I feel left out? Perhaps because nothing I did ever seemed to please them as much as their own joy in each other.

But I am getting away from what I started to say about the incredible thing that happened that day. "Begin at the beginning"; I remember the program analyzer drilling this into us daily at the Collegium, during our course in logical expression. So that is what I shall do: begin at the beginning. Perhaps in the retelling it will all make sense to me at last.

Our Air Cushion Vehicle glided along over the wasted land. Winds blew dirt over what had once been a superhighway, cutting across the Great Plains. At least, that is what this place was once called: the Great Plains. There is nothing great about it now, and it is no longer a plain. Tumbleweeds rolled along like giant beach balls in front of us, bouncing and tossing, following the wind's direction until they were out of sight. It was the most desolate area I had ever seen. Still, as Father kept insisting, it *was* real. No gleaming stilettos of steel pointed at that intense blue sky. No plastiglass domes covered artificial greenery of plastic palms and duroturf. The general flatness of the land made it monotonous, to my eyes at least. It looked as hot and dry as any desert. Vegetation, where it existed, was sparse and scrubby.

Even though the ACV was climatized, I began to feel uncomfortably warm just looking at those miles and miles of nothingness. No wonder my classmates had laughed when I told them of my parents' plans for this deserted part of the world. Still feeling the sting of their ridicule, I said to Father, "What makes you think you can get this place to grow again? Why do you even want to try?"

"Paramecia," Father answered—sometimes he calls me just Para, but usually he uses my full name, since that is the name Mother chose for me—"Paramecia, you have studied about the Eco-War, haven't you?"

What a question! My roboteacher was programmed for world history last year. Father had to know that. "Just ask me anything," I answered. "I took the whole trimester accelerated learning course, complete with memory tapes and audiovisuals. It's embedded in my brain forever."

Father laughed. "Stop complaining! It's easier than the way I had to learn."

"Easier maybe, but not any more fun," I said. "Imagine having to carry all that useless information with me for the rest of my life."

Father's face turned suddenly sober, almost as if I had reached out and struck him. "You may not like learning about the Eco-War, Paramecia, but we can't afford to forget that lesson!"

I prepared myself then for what I knew was coming. I had never understood why mention of the Eco-War always affected Father the way it did. He couldn't have been older than one and a half quadrenniums when it happened.

Father let the ACV drift away from the highway

as he turned his attention to me. "The Great Eco-War!" he said bitterly. "No war has ever been 'great,' least of all that one! Once we became convinced that nuclear weapons were so dangerous that war was no longer a possibility, we got careless. We didn't even notice what was happening until it was too late. Those domed cities of ours were so safe, so insulated. But the really criminal thing about it, Paramecia, was not just that we were complacent and stupid, but that by ignoring the natural world, by continuing to use up and waste and pollute, we actually cooperated with those madmen and their insane plan! If the wildlife was dying, the predatory mammals, the birds of prey, the scavengers, well, it was too bad, of course, but none of us suspected the truth."

"Father, I know all about the eco-destroyers and their plans to conquer the world," I broke in impatiently. "It's embedded in my brain, remember? Why bring up all this ancient history? I know about the droves of mutated jackrabbits, the killer bees, the giant grasshoppers—"

"You know about it," Father cut in, "but does it really mean anything to you? Do you know how scarce wildlife is today? What incredible methods we have to use to bring it back? Paramecia, the whole web of nature was torn apart, the balance destroyed! We killed, we poisoned, we fought back with any weapon we could find, doing even more damage in order to survive."

I gritted my teeth, trying not to let Father know

11

by any outward expression that I had tuned him out. He was like some old soldier of a long-forgotten battle, obsessed with telling the same story over and over. Oh, why had I ruined our pleasure in this day by being negative about his work? Now that I had set him off, he was unstoppable. I loved my father. I wanted to be close to him, but I would never understand this mania of his about the ecology.

"Then came the droughts and famines," Father continued, unaware of my irritation, "and the terrible dust storms, choking every city unprotected by climatized domes. At least we didn't have to worry about the population explosion any more! Inside our protective domes, we survivors piped in desalinated water. We filtered tons of dust out of the air. In some cases, we went underground like moles— but you see what's left of our country, even after all these years!"

Father gestured with with one hand out toward the desolate land surrounding us, then grabbed the wheel as he corrected our drift away from that ruined highway.

"But we won the war!" I said, hoping to bring Father's sermonizing to an end. "I mean, the emergency defense program worked." I didn't think it was necessary to review that program—the new hydroponics, the sea farming with special corps of aquanautic cyborgs. I certainly wasn't going to mention Father's latest obsession—he called it operation Noah's Ark—where they used such measures as cloning, fetal transplants, and genetic reconstruction to build up the decimated animal populations of the world.

"Nobody wins wars, Para," Father said to me grimly. "We survived, that's all. Thank God, the madmen were killed off by their own cleverness! But we must live with the results of their meddling for the duration of our planet. There are so few animals left, we have to go to the zootheriums and the climatized nature preserves to see them."

There it was, the real point of all this lecturing. Exasperated, I cried out, "Animals! Who needs them, anyway? Oh, they're fun to look at, but do they serve any useful purpose? The *true* reason you're so interested in all this is because of Mother —that seems obvious to me!"

"You don't know what you're talking about, Para," Father said sternly. "*All* our efforts are matters of mutual concern. They always have been."

"Oh, I know that. Believe me, I do," I answered. "But still, it was Mother's idea first, wasn't it?"

"No!" Father thundered. He was really angry now. I had never heard that tone in his voice before. It frightened me. There is no rule in our society saying that parents owe any special love or loyalty to their children. What would I do if he just stopped caring about me altogether? I wanted to call back my own stupid words, but it was too late.

"I—I am sorry, Father," I stammered. "I know how much this project means to you, and to Mother—"

"No, you don't, Para, not really. Few young people do, these days. But the land is still here, don't you see? Waiting for us to try again. It is barren, yes—but it isn't hopeless. We've been given another chance!"

I tried to find the right words to say, then. "Father, I know you're a great scientist—Mother, too. I can't tell you how impressed my classmates were when you were preparing for that first test flight toward the possible colonization of Terra Two—"

I broke off in midsentence, realizing there was no way to communicate my feelings about that time of excitement, then failure, when the mission had had to be aborted to assure my parents' safe return to earth. I had been so relieved to see them again, it was like a miracle to me. There would be other flights, and they had promised that on the real colonization flight I was to go with them! Then the project was terminated. I would have to stay in school for practically the rest of my life. All my dreams of the three of us together, one of the first pioneering families in space, were just that: nothing but foolish dreams.

Remembering all that, I turned to Father and pointed to the blue sky above us. "That's where the future is, Father—up there among the planets and galaxies! Not down here on this dying Earth."

"I'm sorry your mother and I didn't quite live up to your expectations," Father said, with only a hint of irony in his voice. Then those amazing eyes of his took on a faraway look as if I weren't even there.

14

The idea was all, to him. "Let me see if I can explain it. Something happened to us up there. It wasn't just the aborted flight. On our way back, we looked out the window of the spacecraft. There was Earth, shining in the infinity of space. Call it space fatigue. Call it homesickness. Call it by that forbidden word 'patriotism,' if you like. We wanted to hold a piece of the earth in our hands and be part of helping it to grow again."

He paused, and I had nothing to say, but I felt sick. Land grubbers! I thought. My parents are nothing but land grubbers.

Seeing the grim look on my face, apparently, Father went on, "Space exploration is exciting to the young, Paramecia. And I understand that curiosity, that need to know. But I have learned that I'm really an earth lover at heart. Why can't you understand? Your mother does."

"Of course—she always understands!" I answered bitterly, anger flaring up inside me again. "What do you care if I understand, anyway? Mother is the only one who really counts with you!"

"Paramecia!" Father shouted. His face told me I had stepped on sacred ground. Then, dropping his voice to a normal tone, he continued, "I realize that hostility toward parents is natural at your age, but you must know you're talking nonsense! Perhaps you need time to calm down. Why don't you put on your alpha-wave headset; listen to a microtape of Beethoven's Pastoral Symphony?"

"Maybe you'd like to shove a little Happiness Pill

down my throat," I shot back, "to restore the chemical balance in my brain, the way some parents do!"

Father shook his head and smiled a sad little smile. "It was bound to happen eventually, this anger of yours. I should have been expecting it. Especially after that long separation, the anxiety we put you through because of the aborted test flight—"

"How could you possibly know how I felt about that?" I cried out. "You weren't here!"

"Paramecia, you're a sensible girl. The beginnings of adolescence can be turbulent at times, but there is great potential in you. Your mother and I have watched you growing up with such interest."

"Oh, really?" I answered sarcastically. "Was I another of your scientific ventures, then? A little private genetic experiment of yours and Mother's?"

"Para! I'd shake you if I thought it would do any good! Listen to me, will you?"

He paused then, and I waited. "Your mother and I listened to the advice of counselors—not to crowd you too much, not to smother you with a foolish protective pride. Finally we agreed to send you away to the Collegium, even though you were only twelve years old. We knew we could contact you at any time, and you would be given holiday periods. Now that it's too late, I wish we had kept you with us. Para, I need you to understand what we hope to accomplish here in this barren place, bringing the earth back to greenness again. I can't force your understanding, but will you at least try to see things our way?"

"Yes, I'll try," I said, pressing my lips together and looking down at my hands. Nothing about this whole conversation had gone right. I *had* wanted to go along on this excursion. I *did* want to understand what my parents were planning to do here, but at that moment I wanted something else more. I wanted my father to stop the ACV, take me in his arms as if I were a little girl, and reassure me that he understood how I felt. Can you imagine anything more ridiculous than that?

I looked out at the deserted, almost Martian landscape, and felt something wrench inside me. Nothing he'd said had really changed anything. Everything here was so dead! It was insane to try bringing it back to life. I turned my head away and said no more.

Suddenly the ACV jerked to a halt and dropped with a jarring thud to the ground. "What is it?" I asked. "Did we hit something?"

"I don't think so," Father answered. "This air cushion we're riding on will go over anything. I could run over somebody, and all they'd feel is the pressure of the air. Rocks, boulders, water holes, swamps, it's all the same to this craft. Must be a power outage." He swung his hatch door open. "I'll check it out, Paramecia. It won't take long."

"May I have a look? I've had the basics of motorization mechanics, you know."

Father looked at me and laughed. "Of course you

have! And if you're at all like your mother, you're probably very good at it."

I should have been pleased. He meant it as a compliment, but at that moment the words sounded unbearably patronizing to me. I would never be as good as Mother, at anything!

I jerked open the hatch on my side of the vehicle and jumped out. "Forget it," I said, "you don't need my help to find out what's wrong with this thing."

Then, right on cue, I heard Mother's voice over the telecom. "What's the matter, Jason? Something's wrong out there. What is it?" Her face appeared on the tiny screen of our control panel.

As small as the image was, even slightly out of focus, Mother's face always made me feel like some kind of mutant. She was so beautiful! Oh, I know there's nothing really wrong with my appearance. My nose comes exactly in the center of my face. My eyes are the same color of blue that my mother and father share. I wear my hair close cropped, like Mother's, and my features, thanks to genetic imprint, are even recognizably similar in some ways. But they lost something in the translation.

Mother never adorns her body with jewelry— except for the Möbius band pendant she wears around her neck, exactly like the one Father gave me. She never paints herself with make-up. Her features aren't remarkable. What is it, then? There is a radiance about her—something I will probably never have.

I don't want to look like her, not really. I want to

look like myself. With these tiny pigmentation spots and my square jaw, I have to admit that my face is an original.

"How did you know something had happened, Athena?" Father asked, as he riveted his attention on the screen. "It's probably nothing serious, just a power outage."

I could have told him how she knew. It was that sixth sense they have between them. Ever since I was a tiny child, I'd seen her stop in midsentence with that puzzled look on her face. "Your father!" she would cry out. "Something has happened!"

And she was always right. Perhaps it was just some jam-up on the passenger conveyor system, which meant he would be delayed getting back to us. Once it was that nearly fatal brush with a giant sea slug, when he was checking out the work of the aquanauts off the coast of Hawaii. When it came to Father, Mother's instincts were at least ninety-nine percent accurate. I suspect he is equally attuned to her. That's how it is with truly pair-bonded people. Two halves of a human puzzle meshing together so closely that they really become like one.

I have never felt that close to anyone, but I know what they feel. And what I felt just then was—left out. I turned away from the ACV and dashed out across the wasteland, kicking up dust as I ran. If Mother had been there she probably would have said, "Better apply a coating of sun filter lotion on your face before you start out, Paramecia. The sun's rays are really strong out here!" But I didn't need her to tell me what to do. I had been away at the Collegium and on my own for over a year. Besides, I did have on my poly-aluminized jumpsuit with its automatic temperature controls. What could possibly happen to anybody out here, anyway?

Then I saw it, a patch of green shimmering through the heat waves. An oasis—out here? Thinking how pleased Father would be if I went to investigate and it proved to be the site of a hidden underground spring, I started running in that direction.

I kept my eyes on that distant spot of color, even though the heat seemed to make it waver and dance in the distance. The closer I got, the more certain I was that this was real and not just some kind of mirage. The green spot grew bigger. I could even make out tree trunks and what looked like bunches of leaves among the branches. But the heat radiation, if that is what it was, grew more definite, too. Almost as if there was a screen of vapors between me and those trees.

To get to where the trees are, I will have to walk directly through that screen, I thought. I hesitated for a moment, then dashed forward. It was not a force field, that was certain, or I would have found myself knocked backward, sprawling, on the ground. No, it was nothing like that. I felt as if I was slipping through a curtain of some thin, cobwebby material, floating through a steam bath that was neither hot nor damp.

I had always done well in my training sessions on

adapting to the unknown. I figured I would need that training if we ever did get to Terra Two. But I had never encountered anything like this before. Such a strange sensation! It was rather pleasant, as a matter of fact. My curiosity overcame any instinct of caution or fear as I forced my body forward.

Suddenly my foot struck solid ground again, landing on springy green grass. Not duroturf, but real grass, a large tuft of it. I touched it just to be sure. The sun was still hot, but there was a hint of moisture in the air now, different from that on the other side of the vapor.

I turned around to judge how far I was from the ACV— It was no longer visible! I had the odd feeling that I was in a totally different place. The screen of vapors had dissolved. In its place I saw a narrow, empty road heading off in the distance.

I am ashamed to admit it now, but as I surveyed this new landscape, instead of feeling lost or frightened I felt an infantile sense of triumph. Like a small child in the first quadrennium of life who runs away from home, I thought, *They'll miss me now that I'm gone. They'll be sorry they didn't pay more attention to me. I don't need them anyway!*

It was this childish reaction of naughtiness, I suppose, that kept me from feeling panic. My time in adaptability training helped, too. I looked down at myself. I touched my small Möbius band pendant, like Mother's—the one Father had given me when I went away to the Collegium. It was still my body in that silver-colored jumpsuit. Those were my boots on my feet. I wriggled my toes just to be sure. Whatever had happened, there had to be a logical explanation.

Well, of course, I thought, fighting off the uneasiness inside me, Father would start looking for me any minute now. If only I had been included in that sixth sense of Mother's she would probably already have him on my trail. But he would notice the green just as I had. So there was no real cause for alarm, I told myself.

If I couldn't get to him, that didn't mean he couldn't come to me. The thing to do was to remain calm.

I pivoted around slowly, surveying the entire landscape, and located the clump of trees I had seen earlier. Somehow, the familiar sight reassured me. I set off purposefully toward those green branches rustling slightly in the wind.

Why act like some helpless servant machine that has just blown one of its components, I thought. An adventure is an adventure, whether it is here or off in the stars someplace. And the greenness looked so inviting after all those miles of dusty desolation.

I entered the clump of trees, then found the reason for its existence. A little sand-bottomed course of water bubbled its way along through the middle of the trees. I recognized willows along the water's edge, and the others appeared to be some kind of poplar or cottonwood. I am not very good at tree identification, though I have been on several excursions to the International Nature Preserves, and

Father used to spend hours showing me pictures of trees when I was little.

I sat down then, resting my back against one of those trees, listening to the quiet sounds of the water, and an even stranger sound to me—the twittering of birds! The quietness rested on me like a soothing hand, better than any alpha-wave headset, better even than listening to Beethoven. The sounds of nature are far removed from my everyday world of teeming cities, carefully programmed studies, constant stimuli of all kinds. My daily life is orderly, purposeful, exciting sometimes—but seldom ever quiet.

Ker-splash! The sudden sound jerked me to alert attention at the possibility of danger. Then, as I saw what had made that noise, I laughed! A slippery-looking green animal, obviously aquatic and about the size of my hand, made a trail of waves in the water directly in front of me, with its large webbed feet—a bullfrog? I thought they had become extinct during the Eco-War. What a prize for Father if I could only catch one!

I jumped up, unzipped my suit, and stripped it off with my boots. I stood there for a moment, feeling as free as some alien creature in a newly created world, my body bare and warm in the dappled sunlight that filtered through the trees. The water was not deep enough for swimming in that particular spot, but as I waded into the shallows I saw that downstream the rushing water had hollowed out a deeper pool. The frog—if it was a frog—had slipped out of sight by now. However, I hoped there might be others. Actually, I welcomed an excuse to refresh myself in the water.

These rocks are slippery, I thought. Better be careful. But careful or not, I soon slipped and tumbled into the water with a splash a hundred times louder than the one the frog had made. It felt marvelous, though, and so did I! I slid and spun my way downstream to paddle about in that deeper pool. Instinctively I brought my hands up into a swimming position. Then, imagining myself an aquanaut, I took a surface dive to the bottom, exhaling bubbles of air as I came back up.

I'm not the earth lover my father is, but being in the water seemed as natural to me as life itself. One of the lessons we all learned from the Eco-War is that when the land fails, the sea will feed and nurture us. Not that I ever intended to join the sea colonizers—I was still fascinated with the idea of traveling the stars, you see. But I shall always be grateful that all of us in the year 2040 are taught from the time we are born to feel at home in the water.

After a while, I stopped splashing about and let my feet rest on the bottom. Actually, even here in the deepest part the water barely came to my shoulders. I paused to catch my breath, and as my eyes swept along the edge of the stream I had the strange feeling I was not alone. There! Just for a second, were those eyes I saw peering at me from a clump of bushes?

I could make out something brownish—hair or fur; I couldn't be certain which—back of the vegetation. It disappeared almost instantly. Perhaps it was an animal. Again I thought how ecstatic Father would be if this place proved to be a natural refuge for supposedly extinct creatures—and I was the one who had stumbled on it! That ought to count for something.

I waded to the opposite side of the pool and climbed out on a large flat rock, to sit as quietly as possible. I hoped whatever it was that I had seen would come back.

Out in the open sunlight, I felt suddenly drowsy, almost as if I had taken some sort of sleep inducer. The sun felt so delicious on my back after the coolness of the water. I stretched out on the large rock to rest.

I certainly didn't intend to go to sleep. The first rule of adaptability training is never to relax your guard. Do not panic, but do not be lulled into a false sense of security, either. I have no defense for my behavior, except perhaps that I *was* tired. I had been in a state of emotional unbalance because of that awful, childish outburst of mine at Father, back at the ACV. And it had been a long trip. For whatever reasons, I could hardly keep my eyes open. I drifted off to sleep.

3

When I awoke, I knew instantly I had done something wrong. Suddenly alert, I rolled over and sat
up. "Oh! Owww!" Gingerly, I touched my gluteus
maximus with my hand, feeling the contrast between the fiery warmth of my backside and the
coolness of my palm. The entire length of my body
from the back of my neck to the soles of my feet
was now toasted a bright, scalding pink. I didn't
need a mirror to tell me that; I could feel it.

I slid back into the stream, trying to soothe away
the fire by cupping up handfuls of the water and
pouring them over my shoulders. It didn't help
much. There was also the alarming realization that

the medical kit was back at the ACV— Well, at least sunburn was something I was familiar with, but how I dreaded putting my clothes back on over that tender skin!

Where were my clothes, anyway? They should have been over there on the other side of the water somewhere. I looked for a glint of silver that would reveal where I had dropped my jumpsuit, but couldn't see anything. I felt panic building inside me, like gorge from a poison in my stomach. Bare and unprotected in this strange place, however peaceful it seemed, I could have some real problems with my adaptability now.

Then I heard an odd noise, a breathy sort of chuckling sound, and a scrabbling around in the green foliage over by the willows. The falling curtain of branches parted slightly, And this time I saw a face. It was a narrow sort of face with a pointed chin. The body beneath that face was smaller than mine and clothed in some kind of nondescript blue garment. Then I saw the glint of silver as the creature grinned at me slyly, held up my jumpsuit, turned away from me, and disappeared.

"Stop!" I shouted. "Those are my clothes! Bring them back." I waited. There was no further movement among the willows, but I heard the sound of footsteps running away from me.

Now what am I to do? I thought. I could feel my self-assurance melting away as wild notions rushed into my brain. Perhaps I had somehow been transported to an alien world. If so, how would I communicate?

If these aliens are all like the one I just saw, I thought, I'm not sure I even want to try. Anger flowed through me—anger and bafflement. What could the creature have wanted with my clothing, anyway? I longed to get my hands on the little imp.

Then I heard a noise like some maddened animal thrashing about unseen in the vegetation. My anger drained away and fear took its place. The sounds grew louder. Finally, I could make out words.

"Blast it, Dingus! Every time I need you, you always run off! Where'd you set them muskrat traps, anyways? Dingus!!" The voice rose to a roar, but it was definitely a human sound, if you could call the swearing and yelling that came next human. "Owww! Goldammit! I sprung one of 'em then for sure! You wait till I get my hands on you!" I felt no curiosity to know the exact reason for such an outburst of bad temper. Whoever this Dingus was, I was glad it was not me.

In the silence that followed, I barely had time to assess the danger of my position before there was a loud blast, explosive and sharp! Instinctively I ducked under the water—just in time. There was a second blast, and something struck the rock beside me in a shower of bubbles and stony fragments!

Muffled through the water, I heard the voice call out, "There's one of them critters now! Dingus, get the sack! I think I got it."

Frantically, I expelled the last bit of air from my lungs, dropping to the very bottom of the pool. Crablike, I crawled to the other side of the rock and remained there, hidden by a protective clump of water grass above me. How grateful I was for my years of breath control training in underwater swim classes! I stayed down at least three minutes.

Finally, the pressure on my chest and a sense of giddiness forced me to break the surface of the water. I took great gulps of air into my lungs, preparing to submerge again. Then I froze, as I looked into another face staring down at me!

It was not the face I had seen before, peering from the willow branches. Somehow I was sure that this could not have been the person doing all that shouting and swearing, either. How could anyone not trust such an open, friendly face? The hair was almost white and rather shaggy; skin, paler than my own; the eyes a startling and familiar shade of blue. It was the grin, however, that disarmed me completely.

I started to speak, but the boy placed a warning finger across his lips, and I remained silent.

"Dingus? Dangblast it, answer me! Is that you?" shouted the voice again.

"Nope. It's me, Shandy," the fairhaired boy answered. "But I seen Dingus running along the road. Looked to me like he was heading towards home."

"Well, blast the little wart, anyways! Shandy, you find a muskrat floating in that water, just remember it's mine! I'll be back directly to claim it." There was more sound as of some elemental force knocking things about, then silence.

"I think I should express my thanks in some way," I said. "I'm not sure what for, exactly. Who was that? And what was that explosion in the water a few minutes ago?"

"That was Jake Murty, the bounty hunter. The less I see of him around here, the gladder I'll be."

"Bounty hunter?" I asked. "What is a bounty hunter?"

The boy looked distressed, then he answered, "Mr. Drucker who owns the land on the other side of the creek here, he hired Jake to kill critters on his property. Besides, Jake gets a extra bounty fee for jackrabbit ears and coyote tails from the county."

"But I heard mention of something else. A muskrat, did he say?"

"If it moves, Jake's got to take a shot at it—it's just his nature," the boy answered. Suddenly he grinned and added, "but you're sure the funniest-looking muskrat I ever did see!"

"I am definitely not a muskrat, whatever that is," I answered. "I am of the genus *Homo sapiens*. So are you, thank the galaxies! My name is Paramecia Foster-Picard. I came out here with my father on an ecological reclamation project—"

The boy looked confused. "I reckon my mind ain't too clear this afternoon. Granny had to give me some of her herb medicine a while ago, because I ran into a swarm of bees. Bee stings make me awful sick. Now, what was that you just said?"

Patiently, I sounded out the words for him again. "I said, 'We came out here on an ecological reclamation project,' and I'm sorry you're not feeling well."

"I'm fine now. Granny's medicine made me a mite fuzzy-headed, and then I started having this terrible dream, till she woke me up—" He broke off, then went on, "What was it you said your name was?"

"Paramecia Foster-Picard."

Suddenly the boy laughed. He threw back his head, his body jiggling with the sound of it. As I stood there in the water, I felt fuzzy-headed myself —not to mention uncomfortable because of my blistered back. Why was he laughing at me?

Apparently seeing my distressed look, the boy stopped laughing. "I reckon it's bad manners to laugh at a person's name. Specially since I got a funny name too. Shandy McShamus Twigg, that's me. Now it's your turn to laugh."

"I have been taught it is uncivilized to laugh at ethnic variations among people, nomenclature included," I answered. "What possible difference could a name make, anyway?"

"Granny says most folks set some store in calling a child by the right and proper name, and I ought to be proud of it, but nobody else around here has a name as downright peculiar as mine—'cept maybe Dingus Murty, and they don't nobody laugh at his name! Least, not in front of his pa. I know—I'll tell you how I come by my name if you tell me how you got yours."

I shrugged. It seemed a witless way to use up

conversation, but if he really wanted to know—
"Well," I began, "at the time I was born, my mother was engaged in research on the paramecian proto-zoans. She was so fascinated with their properties of growth, vitality, and regeneration, she decided to call me Paramecia. Truthfully, I dislike the name, but I suppose I am fortunate at that. Now she is working on the synthesizing characteristics of the Zoochlorella. I prefer Paramecia any day."

The boy laughed uncertainly, then he said, "You know what? I think we ain't even talking the same language. Nothing you just said makes a smidgin of sense to me."

I must remember to reduce my language to its simplest elements, I thought. Tutored as I have been all my life by roboteachers, my speech is standard English, both in grammar and diction. This Shandy spoke some kind of archaic form of the language, almost as puzzling to me as mine apparently was to him. I have not attempted to reproduce it accurately here—only to give some indication of its pattern and tonality.

I began again. "Let me just say, my mother named me after this tiny laboratory animal. Now, how did you get your name?"

"Well, you see," he began, "my ma and pa's both dead, and I live with Granny Twigg. She ain't really my granny, but I reckon she's as good as any ma alive."

"What does this have to do with how you got your name?" I said impatiently. Not that I was really curious, but his habit of wandering off the subject irritated me.

"I was coming to that. Granny tole me Ma's maiden name was Shandy, so she started off with that. Then, of course, my pa's name had to come in. He was a McShamus. Last of all, Granny give me her name, too. So that's how I come to be Shandy McShamus Twigg. Just three last names all strung together. I been teased about it ever since I started school. With that there name of yours, you're liable to get teased a mite, too. If you're figuring to stay around here long, that is."

"Stay here? I hadn't considered—" I broke off, not liking the feeling that came over me then. The panic I had suppressed earlier now pressed in on my brain like a constricting metal band. My rate of breathing grew shallow and rapid. It was an irrational reaction. Behind it, the thought of somehow being trapped in this place. Nonsense! I told myself, and changed the subject.

"I—I think I should get out of the water now, but my clothes seem to be gone. I left them over on the opposite bank there. However, someone appears to have stolen them."

"So that's why Dingus Murty was hightailing it out of here like that!" the boy said. "What'd he want with your clothes anyway? Just orneriness, I guess."

"That was valuable exploration gear he took!" I answered. "Father had it issued to me specially." I grabbed onto the rock and lifted myself part way

34

out of the water, as I added, "But if it's gone, I suppose I'll just have to do without it."

I saw the shocked look on this Shandy's face as he glanced at my chest, then colored a brighter pink than my sunburn. "Lordy lord! You're a girl, ain't you!" he exclaimed. "Just hold on! I'll run and fetch Granny. I reckon she's got some clothes you can wear—something for that sunburn you got, too."

He backed away hastily, then disappeared, leaving me alone again. Fighting off a strong urge to jump out and run away, I tried again to assess my situation.

Somehow, my brain refused to deal with the illogic of it. I had gone through an energy shield, or a vapor screen or something, and now I had lost all contact with life as I had always known it. Everything of my own was gone—except for that Möbius pendant I was still wearing. I pulled it away from my neck and looked at it, remembering Father's words when he gave it to me: "A simple circle represents continuity—unbroken love and all that. But your mother and I like the special twist of the Möbius shape better—unending, unfathomable as time; no beginning and no end. Call it our family symbol if you like." So there it was, a tiny piece of twisted metal, the last remaining proof that I really was Paramecia Foster-Picard, second-year student at the Collegium Pacifica, having been allowed to matriculate early at the age of only three quadrenniums—not because of my parents, but because I had passed every screening test with top scores.

Now, however, that was useless and irrelevant information. I looked around me. This was the world I had to deal with, a world alive with growing things —animals I had not known existed, and humans who seemed almost as strange to me as any alien. I remembered scanning some anthropology A-V course once, about certain places where rural, primitive cultures had survived until the last years of the twentieth century—but those people had supposedly been eliminated by the Eco-War. Rescue teams had been sent out wherever possible, but unless they had made it into the domed cities for refuge, those pockets of humanity had surely been wiped out.

Who then, were these people? Where had they come from? I couldn't deny the evidence of my own senses: a few of them must have survived, somehow. What other explanation was possible? And what was this oasis-like place in the middle of the Great Wasteland?

I resolved to try being a scientist like my father, and to understand this place as well as I could. Adopting a scientific attitude made good sense, if only because it pushed fear away from me.

As the daylight shadows lengthened, I began to shiver and my teeth chattered senselessly—even while my back and arms continued burning as if seared by a hot flame. I had no reason to feel shame about the bareness of my body, but I had to admit one simple truth: the human body is the most vulnerable animal body in the universe. For the first time, I agreed with the theory that it was physical weakness, not superior brain power, that forced humanity up the evolutionary scale. At that moment I would have given anything for a piece of animal skin to wrap myself in.

I clutched my body miserably and shivered again. What would I do if this Shandy did not come back at all?

4

It couldn't have been a quadrant of time later before I saw the boy, Shandy, making his way through the trees again, though it seemed much longer. Following him was another person, with the stooped body of an old woman. More ancient and wrinkled than any elderly person I had ever seen, she was so bent over that she was no taller than Shandy himself. Yet she moved with a wiry toughness, as if she meant by sheer determination to go on living for many more years. She looked like some remnant from a tribe of North American aborigines. Her skin was so deeply tanned, a total contrast to Shandy's

38

blond fairness. Her wispy gray hair was braided and twisted into a bun at the nape of her neck.

"There she is, Gran," Shandy said, pointing at me, then quickly averting his eyes. "Just like I told you. Her name's Para—um, Para-mee-cia. I can't recollect the rest of it, but it was a long one like mine."

"Hey!" Shandy shouted, cupping his hands around his mouth and staring up at the trees so as not to look at me directly. "I'd best not come no closer, you being bare like that. This here's my Granny Twigg." Then he scooted out of sight, leaving me alone with the old woman.

"Many thanks!" I called out, as I climbed over the large rock and stepped out on the bank of the stream. "But there is no need to run away. I wanted to ask you more questions."

"Hush, child!" the old woman said, draping a brightly colored blanket around me. I had never seen a thing like that blanket before. It was made of pieces of material all fitted together into a pleasing design of geometrics. But the nicest thing about it was its warmth. I hugged it to my body gratefully.

The old woman went on talking. "Don't try to call Shandy back now. Couldn't you see he was red clean up to the roots of his hair? You're the first bare female he's seen in all his thirteen years. He don't know whether to stare, or blush, or try to pretend nothing's wrong. I brung you some other clothes— but now that I see that red backside of yours, I reckon the first thing you better get on is some of my soothing ointment."

So saying, the old woman uncapped a small jar and began spreading on a salve, starting at my neck and working downward with deft, soothing strokes. I clutched the blanket to me in front, letting it drop loose in back.

"Well, gal," the old woman went on, "people skin just don't take to too much sun, specially fair skin like you and Shandy's got." Then she cracked a grin, revealing surprisingly good teeth, stained yellow though they were. "Now, if folks was meant to run around naked, I reckon they'd of come into the world with fur coats like the animals."

I knew it was only a joking comment, but I felt goaded into a challenging reply. "But you must have some understanding of human evolution," I said. "Surely this place is not so isolated that no one has read the works of Darwin, the more advanced theories of Huxley, the philosophical views of De Chardin?"

It was reckless of me to ask such a question. Some of those isolated cultures were known to have had rather queer ideas about such things. I knew nothing of these people's attitudes or beliefs. However, the old woman did not seem at all distressed.

"Well, now," she answered slowly, "it never bothered me none to think people's ancestors might of swung around up in them trees. I figure the Bible was telling folks on this earth one thing: that the world and the whole shebang was created; while Darwin and them others was just trying to figure out exactly *how* it all happened." She stopped and pointed her finger at me for emphasis, then went on, "I keep my mouth shut, though, gal! If I was you, I'd do the same—that is, if you're planning to stay around here for a spell."

Again, I felt a shiver of panic at those words, but the old woman went on, "Folks think I be some kind of a witch because of my queer notions. If they heard you talk like that, and seen you running around naked, they'd think you was the Devil's child for sure. Here, let me help you get on this old feed-sack dress of mine." She held up a crude garment of flowered print material, indicating that I was to slip it on over my head. I did so.

Satisfied that I was properly attired at last, she nodded her head and spoke again. "I reckon we'd better head on back to the house now. You hungry?"

"I am nutritionally depleted!" I cried out. "I didn't even bring any protein tablets!"

"If that means you care to have vittles with us, you be welcome," the old woman said. "It ain't much but biscuits and a mess of chicken wings, but I'll make gravy out of the leftover pan drippings. Come on, Shandy, we got company to feed." How she knew Shandy was still within earshot I don't know, but he stepped out of the trees then as we started walking.

The house, when we came to it, appeared to be the simplest and most elemental of shelters. I did notice one large tree spreading out its green branches above the rooftop, offering cool shade. There was no solar heating-cooling system inside—

no electricity, even. One large room served both as kitchen and living space, with two small side rooms for sleeping. A queer-looking device sat in the corner, and from the covered pots on top of it I deduced that it was used for cooking.

My face must have registered amazement, however, as I saw the old woman bend down, open a side compartment, and throw in pieces of wood— obviously to be used for fuel! No one *ever* used wood for fuel, not even in the natural refuges I had visited. Campfires had been declared illegal years before I was born. Wood was simply too precious, almost as rare as that no longer manufactured fuel —what was it called? Oh, yes, gasoline!

I tried to mask my surprise, but the old woman turned around and eyed me shrewdly. "Ain't you never seen a cookstove afore, gal?"

"No, I haven't," I answered honestly.

"I figure your folks must have one of them gas ranges," she said. "I can tell by how you talk, you be city bred. Tell me, would you care to let me know how you come to be here now, or would you ruther wait till we get some food into you?"

The old woman had offered me a chance to think before I answered her question. I needed that chance. Relieved, I took a deep breath and said, "Thank you, I will wait." Without another word she turned back to her work at the stove.

The food set before us on the plain wooden table —it was real wood, not plastic—smelled strange to me, but not unpleasant. The breadstuff appeared astonishingly light in texture, so different from the compressed wafers of food I was used to. I pinched off a piece and popped it into my mouth just as the old woman reached out and ladled some thick, greasy-looking sauce over the rest of the food on my plate. I tried not to wrinkle my nose in disgust. Determined not to offend her, I grabbed my fork and shoved some of the stuff into my mouth. It was surprisingly tasty.

We finished with some kind of sweet fruit concoction—apples, I think, pressed between layers of some kind of flaky pastry. My stomach, unused to such bulky foods, felt uncomfortably full when I stood up after eating. There was another physical need I had to attend to, and something warned me that a blunt request for toilet facilities might be considered improper.

This Granny Twigg, however, seemed to anticipate my needs even before I spoke them. She stood across the table from me, then bent down and handed Shandy a bucketful of water. "Shandy, you go out in front and water my cottonwood for me with this wash water," she said, "and, gal, you best come with me." We walked together to the rear door of the place, and she pointed to a tiny building about two dekameters from the house. "That's the outhouse back there if you be needing it," she said. "We'll talk when you get back."

The less said about the primitiveness of those facilities, the better. There was nothing in my experience to compare it with, but necessity is a strong incentive to adaptation. I did what I had to do and returned to the house.

The evening was warm. We were in the third quadrifid of the year when I started out with Father. That, at least, had not changed with my entry into this place. As we sat together on the porch, the three of us, Granny and Shandy and myself, I knew I would have to face an accounting at last, and try to answer the questions my mind could no longer push aside.

"Well, gal," Granny said, "you be welcome to stay here long as you want, but I reckon we'd like to know a little something about you now."

I groped for the right words. I felt an odd sort of kinship already toward these two because of the way they had accepted me. How much could I tell them that they would understand? How much did I even understand myself?

"Well, I was with my father," I began. "We were traveling across the Great Plains. There was a power failure in our vehicle. Father got out to fix it, and I—well, I wandered off." That much, at least, I was sure of.

"You mean you got lost?" Shandy said. "But I never seen no cars on the road. How far did you come?"

"Your pa must be out of his head with worry, child!" the old woman exclaimed.

I couldn't bring myself then to speak of the curtain of vapors and the disappearance of the ACV. Perhaps I felt that if I didn't admit the truth, it wouldn't be the truth. To be separated from my parents indefinitely, perhaps forever, was unthinkable.

As I struggled with these thoughts, I found the most reassuring words I could think of. "Oh, I know Father is searching for me right now. Perhaps he thought I had simply fallen asleep in the back of the vehicle. As soon as he knows I am gone, he will come back and find me. Of course he will!"

I meant to sound calm and in control of myself. It fooled Shandy well enough, but not Granny. She stared at me shrewdly while Shandy began chattering. "Them Model A contraptions do kind of fall apart onct in a while, don't they? Don't you worry none. You can stay here long as you want to—can't she, Granny? Where is your home exactly? Kansas City? Wichita? You don't sound like you come from anywheres near here. The East, maybe?"

"My home is the city state of the Pacific," I said honestly. From the blank stare Shandy gave me, I could tell this answer meant nothing to him.

After a pause Granny said, "I reckon that'd be California, maybe?"

I recognized the ancient word and acknowledged the similarity of location. "Yes, you could say that."

"Lordy!" Shandy exclaimed. "You sure are a long ways from home! 'Bout a million miles, I reckon."

"Shandy, don't pester her with no more questions," Granny put in. "Time for bed now. I figure you won't mind sleeping in the barn and letting her have your bed."

Shandy grinned.. "Shucks no, Granny. I don't mind."

"No more problems with them bee stings?" Granny asked, a look of fretful concern crossing her face.

Shandy shook his head. "Not even no red bumps. Granny, you are a wonder when it comes to herbs and potions and such."

"But I don't reckon I ought to give you any more of that medicine of mine, Shandy," Granny said, shaking her head from side to side. "You was moaning around and talking crazy and tossing in your sleep something terrible this afternoon when you was taking that nap. Something about all the animals dying— Maybe I better make you a pallet on the floor instead."

Shandy looked pained. "I don't want to talk about them dreams, Granny—I'll be all right," he added. "I kind of like sleeping in the barn anyways."

"Get along with you then," Granny said. As Shandy stood up so did she, and slapped affectionately at the seat of his pants as she added, "There's chores to do in the morning, so don't plan on sleeping too late."

"Come on, gal," she said to me as Shandy disappeared around the corner of the house.

Shandy's bedroom was little larger than a closet. A single bed was the only piece of furniture, except for a chest of some sort with a cracked mirror above it. "You can just sleep in that old dress of mine if you care to," Granny said. "But you best put some

46

more ointment on that sunburn. You might be a bit feverish tonight, too. So here's some willow bark to chew on."

"There is no danger of hallucinatory dreams from this, I trust?" I said suspiciously, eyeing the greenish gray bark Granny had handed me.

She cackled. "This ain't my *strong* medicine, gal. It's got a little salicylic acid in it is all. Same thing they put in aspirin."

The bark was bitter to the taste, but not disagreeably so. The pain on my burned back and legs eased noticeably as Granny rubbed on more of that lotion of hers. Without knowing why exactly, I instinctively trusted these people. Ignorant they might be in some ways—primitive, even. But the way they took strangers into their home spoke of a simple goodness that I never questioned.

Granny's next words, however, immediately put me on my guard again. "Look, you can fool Shandy with that made-up tale of yours," she said. "He's so trusting he'd believe a rattler coiled to strike, if it said it weren't meaning no harm. But something smells of rotten catfish to me. Now let's have the truth, child."

"You may call me Paramecia. That is my correct name," I said, still hoping to delay the course of this conversation. "My whole name is Paramecia Foster-Picard, but just Para will do."

"And Granny will do for you to call me," she said. Then I realized I had already started calling her that in my mind.

"I reckon I be as much your granny as Shandy's anyways," she continued, "least till your folks come to claim you. But where's the true place you come from? Did you run away or what?"

The words were spoken kindly, but she eyed me so directly that I found my words spilling out uncontrolled. "I—I don't understand it, myself! I got out, for a walk. I came through some sort of mist—and when I looked back, our vehicle was gone! That is the truth! What's happened to me?"

"I'll have to think on it," Granny said. "Rest now. Things has a way of making more sense in the morning." She fixed me with a gaze of such intensity, I felt drawn into the depths of those black eyes. "It be a strange story," she continued, "but I've heard stranger. It'll be all right, you'll see."

I cried myself to sleep that night, something I have never done before in my life. I clutched the Möbius pendant Father had given me, as tears coursed silently down the sides of my face and into my hair. I felt like some young sibling separated for the first time from a family unit—on an outing into the International Nature Preserves, perhaps. What was that archaic word? Homesickness, that was it. Homesickness for the place that was in my mind, but I was not sure I could ever return to again. Because for me, such a place might no longer exist.

5

I woke in the night to the murmuring sound of voices and sat up, suddenly alert. I stepped lightly to the open bedroom door and listened again. The voices were coming from the porch outside. Curious, but not wishing to intrude, I moved on into the front part of the house. Looking out the door, I saw dimly the figure of Granny seated in some kind of chair with rockers on the bottom. On the steps below her sat Shandy.

He was speaking: "Granny, I just couldn't sleep so good in the barn with that old hooty owl hollering outside. So, I took me a little walk."

"Tell the truth, Shandy," Granny said sharply.

"You wasn't scared to go to sleep, was you?—Because of bad dreams, I mean?"

"Oh no, Granny! I just wasn't sleepy is all. Then I seen you sitting here. Seeing as how you're wide awake, too, how about telling just one story before I go back to the barn?"

"You don't reckon maybe it's a funny time of the night for storytelling?"

"Nobody tells stories the way you do, Granny. I suppose I never will read a book even half so good. I know folks set some store in listening to their radios around here. But I'd ruther hear your stories any day."

"All right, Shandy. This one seems to be on my mind, so I'll just spin it out . . ."

How can I describe how I felt about that story? Let me see . . . perhaps this would help. One of my classmates at the Collegium was a musician. Instead of using synthesizers, she preferred that quaint instrument, the piano. Her trainer even arranged to move one into the lounge of our living quarters. I found it pleasing to listen to her practice. She would repeat the same music patterns over and over, the tune passing through me almost unnoticed. Then suddenly the melody grew stronger, the notes clearer, surer, as she took command of the music. It became a part of her, flowing, throbbing—alive, almost. Those were rare moments, but real, very real. It was a time we shared together, though she never knew I shared it with her.

That was how I felt listening to Granny while

Shandy sat at her feet, as the tale she was spinning out for him caught me up and held me in its spell. It was an animal story—not one of those ancient, foolish things where animals act and talk like humans, doing things even human beings would not be idiotic enough to do. No, Granny's animals spoke, but in such growls and yips and mews and chirps, the air seemed filled with their cries. It was eerie, yet hauntingly touching.

She told of a time when people shared the world with all the creatures of the forest. Then one of them, Innikuk, a man bent and twisted in his thinking, decided that killing animals was fun, a sport he exploited to gain power and importance.

The birds were slaughtered, first because their meat was tender and delicious, then just because their plumage could be used to adorn the hunters' bodies. Skins of the larger animals became important, so lynx and wildcats were stalked and destroyed.

Unsatisfied, the mad hunter, Innikuk, became obsessed with the notion that coyotes and wolves were the only prey worthy of his attention. They were wily and clever. They were fierce and brave. Only a man who was a real man could match their cleverness with his own. The people must kill them, kill them all, he said.

As the blood lust possessed the people they stalked the land, leaving the winter snow red with the blood of wolves and coyotes maimed and left to die. Then, all the animals mourned. Saddest of all was the long, lonely cry of the coyote, warning of vengeance yet to come, crying out across the barren world.

At this point Granny threw back her head and mimicked the coyote's cry so vividly, I could almost imagine hearing an answering cry off in the distance.

I felt a shiver pass through me, and sudden awe, as Granny continued, "It weren't long," she said, "till folks knew they was truly cursed for what they done. The blood lust was gone then, and they told Innikuk to leave and never come back. But it was too late, you see. Come spring, the deer was thicker than flies buzzing around a carcass. They ate up all the tree saplings along the riverbanks. Deer is regular fools for willow sprouts, Shandy. They stripped the banks clean. Then come the rains. The skies just opened up and poured! Now, they was nothing left on them riverbanks to hold the water back, and there was a terrible flood. Gully washers cleaned out all the river bottom crops. Lots of folks died that year, not just from the flood, but from the famine and sickness that come after.

"The people went into the forest. They called out to the critters to be their friends again, but all they heard was the rustling of the leaves as the critters scurried to hide. 'No way back!' was the call of the hooty owl from the old pine tree. And, 'Too late, too late!' mourned the whippoorwill from his hiding place. So it is, Shandy. So it is even to this day."

"No, Granny!" Shandy cried out. "It ain't true! We let the critters come and go here just as they please. That's how you taught me things was supposed to be."

"This place ain't but a tiny piece of the whole county, Shandy. And they has been a war declared on varmints around here. You know that."

"Why, Granny? Why do folks hate the critters so? It ain't just Jake Murty, though I reckon he's the worst. It's the blood lust, ain't it? It reminds me of that nightmare I was having this afternoon—when they wasn't no animals left in the world, hardly at all! Nobody cared, even! But I care—"

"Hush!" Granny soothed. "It was just a dream. Don't fret yourself over it."

"But I ain't never harmed no animal!" Shandy went on. He seemed distraught almost to the point of hysteria.

"Shandy, that was just a story I took a notion to tell you," Granny said. "I'm sorry I done it now. I reckon it was a mistake, like giving you my medicine that brung on the bad dream—I must be getting addled to do such things!"

"Now Granny, the dream's all gone away now! And I was awful sick from them bee stings. Tell the truth—you thought I was going to die, didn't you?"

"Shandy—" Granny began, but he cut her off with his own words.

"It's just too bad you can't mix up some potion that would make the blood lust go away!"

"Shandy, listen to me!" Granny commanded.

"Truth is, most folks around here don't hate the critters. They're just so used to scratching and fighting nature every time they's a drought or dust storm, or a rain coming at the wrong time, after a while everything starts looking like a varmint to them. Lord knows, Shandy, they's millions of jackrabbits out there!"

"If folks hadn't hired Jake Murty to kill off the coyotes, then we wouldn't have so many jackrabbits. I truly do believe, Granny, I like animals better'n people."

Granny chuckled. The small expression of mirth came from deep inside her throat. "According to what that gal, Paramecia, says, we all be blood relatives to the critters, anyway." Suddenly she swung around in her chair and stared at me. Even in the darkness, I saw the glint of her eyes. "Well, Para, ain't that so?"

Startled, I stammered out the first words that came into my mind. "How—how did you know I was standing here? You—you never looked at me. You never gave any sign."

"How I knew it ain't important," Granny answered. "It just come to me, that's all."

"But I—I wasn't really spying on you. I just wanted to listen to your story."

Shandy laughed then. "You'll just have to learn about Granny's ways, Para. I didn't know you was standing there. But Granny—well, I never got by with ary a thing when I was growing up. Steal a cookie out of the crock in the kitchen, and she knew it. Sneak away to go splashing in the creek, Granny was there at the door 'fore I ever got away. It's just her way, that's all."

I wasn't ready to deal with Shandy's hint of super-normal abilities, not at this hour of the night, so I answered, "At any rate, I'm sorry I intruded on your conversation. Now if you will excuse me—"

"No, don't go!" Shandy protested. "Come and sit awhile with us if you care to."

There was a hint of welcome coolness in the night air as I sat down beside Shandy on the steps. I looked up and saw the most brilliant display of stars I had ever seen, brighter far than I ever remembered them. It was comforting to me that the constellations were familiar: Ursa Major and Minor, the Pleiades, Sirius shining like some brilliant jewel, and the total spectrum of the Orion constellation. Whatever had happened to me, I was still at home on my own planet. The stars told me that much.

We did not speak for a while. Words seemed unnecessary somehow. I felt such a sense of belonging and tranquillity, I didn't want to break the mood. Yet I was the one who broke the silence finally. Remembering Shandy's remarks earlier, I said, "You mentioned that the animals are allowed to come and go here as they please. Are there many different kinds of animals? Would it be possible for me to see them?"

"Just keep your eyes and ears open," Granny answered. "I reckon you'll see about as many as you got time for. Of course, about all you've got to do to scare up a jackrabbit is chuck a rock at the nearest plum thicket."

"Granny, I know!" Shandy exclaimed. "If she wants to see critters— You reckon the rabbits might be dancing up on the road tonight?"

"Dancing?" I asked. "I suppose you are referring to some sort of mating ritual?"

Granny chuckled. "Truth to tell, Para, they don't nobody know why the rabbits act the way they do sometimes. Lordamercy! If I didn't know better, I'd reckon they must of been drinking thorn-apple tea."

"And there is a chance I could see this for myself?" I said. I didn't really believe such a thing was possible; still, in this incredible place, who could tell?

"Can we, Granny?" Shandy said. "Couldn't we just go and have a look-see?"

"I reckon it's a piece of foolishness in the middle of the night like this," Granny answered tartly. "Shandy, we don't even know if they'll be out tonight."

"They'll be there; I can feel it," Shandy answered, a sort of pleading conviction in his voice.

I found myself puzzled by the intuitive level at which these two seemed to order their lives. Fascinating! I thought; I must remember to take notes of some sort.

Granny measured her words carefully as she answered, "I reckon you can go, but . . . something don't seem right about it. Never mind! Take the electric torch from the barn, Shandy, but don't you stay out too long, you hear me?"

As Shandy and I started up the pathway toward the road, it occurred to me I had never been out of my domicile for a walk at this hour of the night. Where would I have gone, anyway? Out to ride aimlessly up and down on the conveyor systems?

An odd sort of anticipation gripped me, as Shandy crouched down in the ditch running parallel to the road and motioned me to do the same. For one who was normally so talkative, he seemed strangely silent as he moved his head alertly from side to side, listening.

At first I heard nothing. Then a sort of muffled thumping sounded in my ears. Shandy switched on the light. Almost immediately the beam caught the figures of animals—dozens of them, all over the roadway. They were jackrabbits, no question about it. Though I had seen pictures of them, I was astounded by the actual size of those ears. I stared at them, these creatures who had come so close to ending the natural life on our planet, and shuddered involuntarily. I had asked eagerly to come along. Yet, seeing these creatures up close like that gave me a strange feeling. I knew much more about their potential for destructiveness than Shandy did, apparently. As I watched them, however, my instinctive fear changed to a sense of wonder.

They were fascinating. No zoothcrium animal could possibly have displayed such sheer animal exuberance. Incredible! Perhaps they *had* ingested some sort of hallucinogen. I knew nothing of thorn apples, but peyote? Ergot? Who could tell? The animals jumped and leaped over one another. They cavorted about in large circling groups. If I hadn't seen it for myself, I wouldn't have believed it.

Then I noticed two half-grown specimens who seemed to have lost the antic mood of the rest of the group. Off to themselves, they glared at each other, head on. However, their eyes were so far to the sides of their heads, the effort made them appear comically cross-eyed. I watched in amazement as the two rabbits backed away from each other and then began charging forward at top speed! Just as they would surely have cracked heads, one of them suddenly leaped into the air while the other swept past underneath. The loser in that crazy battle of wits was several feet away before he stopped and shook his head in confusion. When I heard the soft chuckling beside me, I knew Shandy had been watching, too.

Then, the battle over, the pair hopped back into the larger group of rabbits. They began somersaulting over the top of a large adult who, catching their spirit of playfulness, rose on his great padded feet and hurtled himself into the air. It was an astonishing burst of energy.

Suddenly an explosive sound ripped through the silence—"Blam!" I jumped and covered my ears, but my eyes saw the body of that large rabbit stiffen and then fall limp onto the ground. Scurrying rabbit feet kicked up the dust of the road as rabbits rushed pell-mell, hurtling over the ditch where we crouched!

Shandy must have switched off the torch light, for we were suddenly in darkness. I felt a single furry body brush past me as the rest of the rabbits escaped, scattering into the night.

There was a strange, unnatural quiet then. I waited with a growing sense of dread to see what would happen next.

The light flooded back on, and Shandy stepped into the roadway. I heard his soft intake of breath as the light focused on the dark form lying still in the dust. A glistening puddle of blood spread out upon the ground. Then one hind leg jerked and quivered for the last time. Shandy bent down. I heard a strange sound, a stifled whimper, almost like that of an animal's cry, and I knew the sound came from Shandy.

"Hold it right there, Shandy Twigg!" shouted a voice from the darkness. "I got me one pair of bounty ears, at least. So you just keep hands off! If you hadn't switched off that light so fast, I'd maybe got me a couple more."

"You murdering devil!" Shandy yelled. "Jake Murty, I hope every nickel you make on bounties has a Judas curse on it!"

For answer, the hulking form of Jake Murty stepped into the light. I didn't see the face, for his back was toward me. But I watched, horrified, as he stepped on the limp body with one booted foot. Bending down, he grabbed the ears, and with the knife in his free hand slashed around them, letting the mangled body fall back into the puddle of blood.

I shuddered and turned away. Then I heard the sound of scuffling and jerked my head back. Shandy had dropped the light, its beam pointing off into empty space. In the half light above the fallen torch, I saw Shandy pummeling Jake's huge form with his fists. "Stop it! Stop it! Stop it!" he cried.

With a swift cuff of his hamlike hands, Jake knocked Shandy away from him. "Crazy! That's what you are! Both you and that Granny of yourn. You better leave me be, or I'll thrash you till you can't sit down!"

"You just stay away from our place, Jake, you hear?" Shandy blazed back.

Jake snorted. "Hunh! You'd think that little old patch of ground on the far side of the creek was some kind of national game preserve. Varmints all over the place, breeding and spreading like maggots! But folks around here is getting sick of it, Shandy Twigg. We'll clean that nest out one of these days, you just watch!"

Shandy didn't answer. Covering his ears, he ran, stumbling, back toward the house. Jake looked down at the dead rabbit, unaware that I was in the ditch watching. Now, for the first time, I saw his features. "Brutish" is the only word I can think of to describe them. Mean little eyes, a bulbous nose, and fleshy jowls covered by a stubble of beard. I know one shouldn't judge character by appearance, but it was a singularly unattractive face. I refuse to use the word "degenerate," for I knew nothing of his ancestry, but there was something animal about him—animal in the worst sense of the word.

Jake Murty's next actions did nothing to change my impression of him. He suddenly kicked viciously at the rabbit carcass and muttered something that sounded like, "Buzzard bait!", then stalked off up the road.

I retrieved the light and stood there, not moving. What kind of place had I come to? The hard cruelty of a man like Jake Murty was incomprehensible to me. If it was true what he said, that other people were in sympathy with him, this was a terrible place —no matter how peaceful it had seemed at first. And yet—and yet—if the rabbits were a threat, if they *had* started to overpopulate again, could the people be blamed for taking whatever desperate measures might be needed? My mind held no answers, only confusion. I had the sudden urge to run and run and run until I somehow escaped from this place.

Instead, I turned and started back toward Granny and Shandy's house.

6

No matter how bad the night, morning always comes, somehow. When the sun started to break over the horizon and send its rays into my window, I felt almost as if some primordial dawn on a new planet had begun. The air seemed cleaner than I could ever remember. Yet it was also heavy with smells I could not identify. It had never been filtered, processed, or decontaminated. It was simply fresh air. I breathed it in thankfully, as I lay there on Shandy's bed. But the bad memories of the night before didn't go away.

I sat up when I heard the clatter of dishes in the main room. Granny was preparing food again, and like the summons of the buzzer commanding us to rise and swallow our morning supply of nutrients, those kitchen sounds told me I was expected at the breakfast table.

I got up. Then, eyeing my appearance in the mirror with distaste, I smoothed a few wrinkles out of Granny's old dress with my hands.

She was alone when I came into the room. No sign of Shandy about anywhere. As if anticipating my unasked question, Granny spoke, "I reckon Shandy's too upset for breakfast this morning. So I figured I'd leave him be. He's too tenderhearted, that boy. It'll kill him one of these days, I reckon. It's the pure cussedness of it that he can't stand."

"But why—why is Shandy that way?" I asked. "Jake Murty loves killing animals! He says other people here feel the same way he does. Why are you and Shandy so different?"

Granny eyed me for a moment without speaking, as if she was considering her answer before she spoke. "I reckon we just see things different than most folks is all. Rabbits can be pestiferous, and that's a fact. Too bad Jake saw fit to kill off all the coyotes around here."

Granny's words struck a responsive chord in my memory. "Is it true then, that the rabbits are a threat?" I said. "Could it be possible for them to reach such numbers that they overran the whole country? They did that once, you know—" I broke off as I saw the strange, alert look on Granny's face—not puzzled, really, but expectant. As if she waited for some clue that would solve a mystery she did not fully understand.

Oddly, I had never yet said anything to this seemingly ignorant old woman that she did not respond to instantly and answer with a sharp intelligence. She did not break the pattern now. "Maybe you better tell me about that other time," she said. "They was a danger, you say—a rabbit danger to the whole country?"

Such total isolation was incredible to me. Everyone knew about the great Eco-War! How could Granny not have heard of it? She was old, much older than my father. It had been the single most important event in his life. "Surely you have some memories of the Eco-War!" I said. The rest of my words tumbled out almost as if a triggered response had been set off. It was an instant history lesson, played out directly from those memory tapes of my roboteacher.

Granny took it all in without a word of interruption. When I finished, she answered with controlled anger in her voice. "Folks don't never learn, do they? They's always wanting to tame nature so's it'll serve them, and going about it all wrong! Instead of trying to learn how ever' living thing needs ever' other living thing, they just look around and say, 'We don't need that. It don't serve no purpose at all. It's a pest, a varmint. We gotta get rid of it.' But worst of all is when they say, 'I can use that. I can use up ever' bit of it. It's my world! I'll do what I want, and they ain't nobody can stop me!'

Sure enough, one day it's all gone, and it's too late to bring things back the way they was before."

It might have been my father speaking; the words mirrored so closely his own ideas. Yet when Granny said them, I listened, really listened, to what she was saying, as if they were the words of some wise teacher. Words to hang onto and never forget.

I got up and began pacing about the room. Even if these people were remnants of a primitive culture, somehow untouched by the events of the last thirty years, they were not ignorant savages—at least not all of them. Already I felt a strange kinship toward Granny and Shandy, as if they were part of my family, almost. Oh, not that I had the same feeling toward them as toward my parents—of course not! I owed them no lasting loyalty. I was like a prisoner here, in a way, though that was certainly not Granny and Shandy's fault.

My emotions were in such turmoil that I turned back to Granny and shouted out the first words that came into my head. "Where did you come from? What makes you and Shandy so special?"

"I come from the Ozark hills, Paramecia. So long ago I can scarce recollect it. All my folks was dead, so I moved on and ended up here in Kansas. When I found Shandy's ma, Shandy's pa was already dead, and Shandy not even born yet. I was some good at midwifing, but not good enough I reckon. Though, Lord knows, I done all I could for the poor thing when her time come. I reckon Shandy's told you we ain't really related. But family's family, however it happens. I'm all he's got, and he's all I got. It's the feeling that matters. Don't you think so?"

I felt somehow embarrassed by such an open expression of feelings, and could not find the right words to answer. I changed the subject instead. "Since Shandy isn't here right now, I'd be glad to help out with his work. But, uh, would you mind if I didn't wear this dress of yours? Perhaps some old things of Shandy's would do just as well."

Granny laughed. "I reckon you're right. Pants on a gal don't bother me none. But it might not set too well with some folks around here."

"Sexual difference has little to do with the clothing one wears," I answered. "I do think Shandy's clothes would be more like what I'm used to." I didn't mention my stolen jumpsuit, but I wished heartily there were some way to find it and get it back.

"How's your sunburn feel this morning?" Granny asked.

"I—I hardly noticed it!" I said, touching my shoulders. Before, an accidental overdose of the sun's rays might have troubled me for days. Blistering and peeling, my skin would surely not have restored itself this quickly. "That ointment of yours is really quite remarkable," I said. "If you don't mind, I would like to have a sample for Mother to run a chemical analysis on. I know she'd be impressed."

"Take it, if it pleases you," Granny answered. She stood up and moved toward Shandy's bedroom. "I'll just fetch you a pair of Shandy's bib overhauls and a old shirt now," and she went on out of the room.

It's odd the way the mind works, I thought, beginning to pace the room again. I talked of taking some ointment back to my mother, yet I had no idea how that was to be accomplished. I determined to go out and do some exploring as soon as I changed my clothes. There *had* to be a way to get back to where I had left the ACV. It was a logical assumption. If one arrived at a certain place, then there must be a way back from that place.

Suddenly my attention was arrested by an object fastened to the wall near the stove. I approached it curiously. It looked vaguely familiar, somehow. Of course! I had seen a very similar thing in the Archival Museum of Antiquities. It was a rare, old-fashioned, paper calendar. The year 1934 was clearly marked on it. Did that year have some special significance to Granny? I wondered. Her birth date, perhaps? I did some brief mental computing— Impossible! That would have made Granny over a century old. Still, I decided to ask her how she had come by such a treasure.

Then I looked more closely at the calendar. I touched the new, shiny-slick paper, a pastoral scene painted on it of colors a shade too bright to look real. No crumbling of the edges. No fading, no discoloration. The month was marked there on a separate section—MAY—and the date again, 1934. Some of the pages had apparently been removed. Otherwise, the thing was in absolutely mint condition!

It must have cost a fortune. But how—?

A sudden terrible suspicion hit me like the shock wave from a crowd immobilizer gun. Frantically, I looked around the room for some other evidence to confirm or deny that awful suspicion.

There, under a pile of wood next to the stove, I spotted another ancient thing. I pulled it out, a slightly yellowing section of newspaper. This I had never seen before, not even in the Archival Museum, except on microtapes, of course. Printed across the top, the words: *Farmer's Weekly Journal*, and again a date—May 3, 1934!

That vapor screen I had passed through—it had been some kind of time warp! The shock stunned my thought processes. I stood there unable to move —unable to think—

Then from outside there was a scream—"Granny!" My muscles jerked involuntarily, and almost instantly Shandy came running in. "Where's Gran?" he called. "They done it! Oh, they killed 'em—every single one!"

"The rabbits?"

"No, the prairie dogs!" Shandy cried, his voice a keening wail of anguish.

Granny hurried back into the room. "Now just hold steady there, Shandy," she said. "I told you I seen a couple of ferrets out by the prairie-dog town the other day—"

"No! They been poisoned! There's dozens of prairie dogs lying stiff on the ground out there. Come see for yourself!"

They were all dead. I took in the scene with a kind of special horror, not quite believing what I saw. I had never seen a live prairie dog, though I remember at one time viewing a film clip of those playful, charming creatures, now extinct. I mean in my own time, of course.

My mind still had not grasped the reality of living in two different time tracks. But it was cruelly ironic that this once-in-a-lifetime chance to view, firsthand, all these delightful creatures, should be blighted by what I actually saw.

I stood with Granny and Shandy, looking out across the pastureland. Some of the prairie dogs had dropped close to their hills. Some were scattered at random through the grass. Only one seemed to be still alive. I bent down to look more closely. The small animal quivered, but his body seemed rigid, as if his muscles had begun to turn to stone. On the ground close to the body I saw small, dark-red kernels of some kind of grain, and then a whole cluster of them on a stalk. I picked up the stalk, puzzled.

Granny stared at what I held in my hand and yelled out, "Strychnine poison! Somebody's been dipping Kaffir corn in strychnine. Look! The stuff's scattered all over for bait. No wonder they's all dead!"

Something clicked in my mind then, and I remembered Jake Murty yelling, "We'll clean that nest out one of these days, you just watch!"

At almost that exact moment, I saw something

move at the corner of my vision. I jerked my head and saw a smallish figure darting away across the horizon.

"It's Dingus!" Shandy yelled. "Come on! Let's catch him. He knows something about this. He's bound to!"

We raced out of the pasture, Shandy and I. I scarcely noticed where we were headed. I was too intent on keeping up with him, and was glad I had taken time to change into the overalls Granny had given me—at least I wasn't hampered by a skirt. Occasionally I caught a glimpse of somebody running on ahead of us, but Shandy seemed as sure of where he was going as if he followed a well-marked trail.

I am a fairly competent runner. It is one of the skills encouraged by the Collegium, as it keeps the body well exercised and releases a certain amount of nervous tension as well. However, I suspect Shandy and Dingus must have been chasing jack-rabbits across those fields from the time they were small children. Shandy was far ahead of me when I finally had to stop and regain my breath.

As I looked about me at this unfamiliar terrain, it suddenly struck me—I might almost be back on the Great Wasteland again! Plowed fields stretched out in front of me, marked off by sagging wire fencing. There was a desolate-looking two-story gray house made of rotting wood, surrounded by debris and tumbleweeds, and another dilapidated building off to one side. Surely no one lives in such a place, I thought. Granny's house was small and anything but luxurious, but it was livable. There was also that large cottonwood tree Granny took such patient care of. This place, on the other hand, was simply unfit for humans—or so I told myself. However, that was exactly where Shandy was heading.

As we drew nearer, I saw a couple of small children with grimy faces playing among the piles of junk. One of them tugged at the collar of a skinny, long-eared hound who then snapped viciously at the child, but missed.

"Here, Rosie! Leave that dog alone!" Someone called from the porch. I looked up. A gaunt woman of indeterminate age stood there, holding a pale infant in her arms.

Shandy didn't hesitate, but marched to the foot of the steps. "Mrs. Murty, you seen Dingus around here anyplace?"

She answered in a tired, whining voice, "He ain't here, Shandy. I can't keep track of him, nohow. Always off with his pa somewhere. Lord knows, I could use him for the chores around here."

"Do you mind if we have a look around, ma'am?" Shandy asked politely.

"Suit yourself," she answered, shrugging. Then she turned away and moved back into the house.

Shandy headed toward that ramshackle building off to the left. It was a barn, I suppose, though hardly a decent place to house livestock. As we approached, I heard noises—the sound of scuffling, muffled curses, then a whimpering sound.

Shandy stepped quietly toward the back of the barn, and I followed. Jake Murty had his back turned toward us. He was so intent on what he was doing that apparently he had not heard us. Stretched out on the ground in front of Jake was what looked to me like the body of a young coyote. It was dead now, but I noticed with a shock that there was a wire wrapped around the creature's muzzle. Perhaps that was to keep it from biting; but it must have died of slow starvation, judging from the emaciated condition of the carcass. One of its hind legs was badly mangled, from shooting or a trap. I had no idea which.

Slinking along on the ground as if he wanted to disappear into the earth was a half-grown pup, some kind of gangly hound, probably an offspring of that dog I had already seen in the front yard. The pup whined pitifully as Jake continued yelling at him, "Come on, you! Kill it! Rip it open!" Jake dug his boot into the coyote's side. "Get a taste of coyote blood, you dang fool. Got to learn you to be a good varmint killer like your ma!"

The dog cowered there, trembling; so Jake cursed and aimed his next kick at the dog. "Get on out of here then, you mangy whelp!" The dog took off, faster than the speed of light, almost. I watched him disappear over a slight rise at the horizon's edge and thought, if he's smart, he'll never come back.

Jake turned around then, and saw us standing there. "What you doing here?" he asked curtly.

"Jake," Shandy answered, "somebody put poison out on our property and killed our prairie dog critters! I know it was you. If it wasn't you, it was Dingus, and I mean to put a stop to it."

"How you aiming to do that?" Jake sneered.

"I ain't never killed a living thing. I don't even know how to shoot that old gun of Granny's, but I can learn. If you ever set foot on our property again I'll blow your head off! I reckon that's all I got to say, but just don't you forget it!"

Jake stared openmouthed for a second, then he threw back his head and laughed. "Danged if I ain't got me a wildcat by the tail here. You better watch out for them old guns, Shandy McShamus Twigg. Most of 'em got a kick like a mule. Haw! Blow my head off, will you?"

Shandy stood silent for a second. Tears of anger glistened at the corners of his eyes. Then he shouted, "You won't never laugh at me—never again! I mean it. I'll kill you—I will!"

"I thank you for the warning," Jake answered, "and I'll see you at the church next Friday when we get together for the varmint kill. If you gonna take up killing, you better start with a club 'stead of a gun. Now get on out of here. Before I lose my temper!"

7

While this emotional exchange of words had been going on, a crowd had gathered. A row of children in stair-step sizes had quietly arranged themselves to one side of where Shandy and I stood, and now Mrs. Murty joined them with the baby, the child sucking intently on his thumb. One of the larger children looked familiar to me—that narrow face and pointed chin, the sly glint of those eyes. Of course! It was Dingus Murty, looking every bit as impish as before, when I had seen him peering through the willow branches. He winked at me slyly, as if this whole incident had been planned especially for his amusement. An unreasoning anger rose inside me. I felt as if I wanted to grab him and shake him violently. There was something so—so malicious about him.

Granny was there, too. I had missed seeing her until I heard her call out, "Jake Murty! Before you start ordering Shandy around, you got me to answer to." As she stepped through the crowd of children, I saw that she had some kind of ancient weapon hoisted over her shoulder.

"Well, I reckon we got the whole tribe here now, ain't we?" Jake answered sarcastically. "You figuring on starting a feud, maybe?"

"They is a word for varmints like you," Granny said, ignoring Jake's question as she pointed a finger at him and squinted one eye. "I ain't going to use it, though, not in front of children. This gun here, Shandy don't know how to use it—but I do!"

"Then why don't you use it on them pestiferous prairie dogs you got down there?" Jake asked. "They ain't good for nothing, except tearing up pasture and making livestock fall in those holes they's always digging."

Granny shouted back, "That's foolishness! None of your stock is going to be falling into any holes on my property anyways, Jake! But you could of killed my cows, putting out poison like that."

Mrs. Murty spoke then. "Granny, I don't think you ought to go about saying such things 'less you got proof. Jake's just doing his job the best way he knows how. I could wish for him to be a better farmer, but I reckon he knows his business when it comes to killing varmints. Jake, tell her you never put no poison out— You didn't, did you?"

"Be quiet, woman! This don't have nothing to do with you," Jake answered.

"Why don't you ask Dingus what he knows about all this?" Granny said.

I watched Dingus then, as the grin disappeared from his face and his eyes darted from side to side like a trapped animal's, searching for an escape.

"Shut up, old lady!" Jake said. "And get off my property 'fore I turn my dogs loose on you! I take care of my own kids without no help from meddling old crazies like you!"

"Jake, I ain't leaving till I have my say," Granny answered, with cold determination in her voice. "Even if Dingus did throw out that poison Kaffir corn, I know who must of put him up to it. Come to think of it, shooting is too good for the likes of you! You better watch what you do from now on! There's secret hexes and potions you never even dreamed of, Jake Murty!"

"What do you mean, old woman?" Jake blustered. "I ain't scared of you!"

"I've seen folks get sick without nobody ever knowing the cause," Granny answered, just the slightest hint of menace in her voice. "Grown men, weak and sickly like newborn calves, because they's eaten up with fear from inside." Then that bony finger of Granny's came out again. She aimed it at Jake and said, "Stay away from our place. I'm warning you!"

76

Jake Murty began to turn pale. He rubbed his hands together, then wiped them on his pants legs. "I don't scare that easy, you old witch woman!" he yelled. But he was scared—terrified, in fact. "What makes you think you got a right to take the only other decent piece of farmland left around here, besides Drucker's, and turn it into a breeding place for every varmint that runs or hops or crawls? I suppose next thing, you'll be damming up the creek so's we can't get the use of the spring water, neither!"

"I'd never do that, Jake, and you know it!" Granny blazed back. "It ain't spring water that makes the difference. Folks all over are killing the land by all this plowing. Then there comes a dust storm or a hard rain, and away goes all the topsoil. It ain't varmints that makes the trouble, it's people!"

"Dang it all! If you had your way I guess we'd have to start shooting *people* to protect the *animals* from our murdering ways!" Jake answered. "People is the important thing here. Feeding them, covering their bodies with clothes— Why, out here in Kansas we can't even get cool shade from the hot sun till we get rabbits to stop stripping bark off every young tree that's planted."

I thought of Granny's cottonwood, and started to say something. Before I could get the words out Mrs. Murty spoke up. "That's right, Granny. Jake's got a bunch of kids to feed here. How's he going to do that when the rabbits and prairie dogs won't stay out of the wheat fields?"

I looked around at those dirty-faced, poorly cared for children and blurted out the first words that came into my head. "Has no one here ever heard of birth control? Too many babies can be as bad as too many rabbits! The solution to your problem seems obvious to me."

There was a shocked silence. Then Mrs. Murty spoke. "Hush your mouth, child! It ain't proper to talk of such things!"

"Who's this one?" Jake called out, pointing at me as if I was some kind of alien insect. "I ain't never seen her before. Or is she a he? I can't rightly tell for sure."

"Her name's Paramecia," Granny answered. "She's staying with us for a spell."

"Taken in another stray brat, have you?" Jake sneered. "Then, old woman, you better tell her to keep a decent tongue in her head!"

"If you have criticism of my words, you may tell me," I answered. "I was *not* being disrespectful, only logical. An overcrowded world is a terrible thing! It can bring famine, disease, poverty, all sorts or social ills."

"The Lord told us to be fruitful and multiply!" Jake intoned, as if this was the absolute final word on the subject.

"If God told people anything at all," I answered, "He did not tell them to breed more children than they could decently care for. I would be ashamed of using sex in such an irresponsible manner!"

"Filth!" Jake roared. "All you kids, cover up your

ears so's you won't have to hear such sinful words. She's talking blasphemy!"

"When did you get such a dose of religion, Jake?" Granny said sarcastically. "Only time I ever seen you at church was when they was planning another varmint kill."

Jake was livid with anger. "I've had me enough of this! They ought to be a law against crazy old women having the care of kids like that. No telling what notions you'll be putting in their heads next! Where'd this one come from, anyways?"

"I seen her before, Pa!" Dingus said, stepping out in front of his brothers and sisters. "I seen her down by the creek the other day. She was naked as a jaybird!"

There was an intake of breath from Mrs. Murty and some of the children, as if Dingus had said something really shocking. No one spoke, however, until I moved toward Dingus and said, "Yes, and you stole my clothes, too! I would appreciate it if you would return them at once."

"Dingus!" Jake roared. "If you got anything that belongs to that gal, you best give it back before I blister your behind! We don't have no cause for stealing around here."

"I never done it, Pa!" Dingus protested, his eyes wide as he shook his head back and forth. "I never done no such a thing! She's crazy, that's what! I seen her splashing and dancing around down there by the creek, without no shame at all— But that's all, I swear it!"

It was a most convincing display of innocence. At least, it fooled Jake. "I heard all I want to hear from the three of you!" Jake roared. "Now get off my property! If any one of you ever sets foot here again, I'll have the law on you!"

On the way way home we were silent, the three of us. As we walked along the hard-packed dirt road, I noticed Shandy looking sideways at Granny. She noticed it too, apparently. Finally she said, "Out with it, Shandy. You been eyeing me like a hound-treed possum ever since we left Jake's. What is it?"

"Granny, you ain't really planning to put a hex on Jake Murty, are you?"

Granny cackled. "No more than you was planning to shoot him! I ain't about to get sent off to jail for killing the likes of Jake Murty—but I just might have me a try at scaring him to death!"

"But, what you said about secrets and potions—"

Granny cut off his words as she answered, "I figured they was a good chance Jake might be superstitious, at least about some things. I'd use that against him if I had to, to keep him away from our place, but that's all."

Shandy smiled in apparent relief. Then Granny began to cackle again. "I don't hold with killing for sport nor pleasure. I always figure, if you kill it you got to eat it. And I ain't about to eat no human carcass, 'specially not Jake Murty's!"

"Speaking of killing," I said, "there was one thing Jake Murty said I didn't understand at all. Something about a 'varmint kill' at the church, and using clubs instead of guns—"

Shandy grimaced and said, "You tell her about it, Granny. I—I just can't."

Granny's eyes started to take on an outraged look as she began speaking. "They call them varmint kills, but mostly they're for rabbits. All the folks will be gathering at the church this Saturday. The women will be fixing food for when the menfolks get back from the slaughter. And that's what it is, Paramecia, a slaughter. First they put up a semi-circle of chicken wire—a long one, maybe close to a quarter of a mile. Then the men and boys all line up and start driving all the animals towards that chicken wire. They beat on the ground and make a terrible racket. By the time they get up to the fence, the line is a solid wall of men and boys, with the animals trapped there along the chicken wire. I seen it once, Para, and once was enough for me. The noise'd like to bust your eardrums—the squealing of the animals, the shouting of the men. It's a wonder they don't hurt each other, they get so excited. If it's a really big kill, sometimes they might be as many as two, three thousand animals dead when it's over. And if it's not so good, maybe they'll set that fence up another place and try again the next day."

"But what do they do with the animals?" I asked, horrified.

"The ears they take for bounty money. Part of it

goes to Jake Murty for figuring out the whole thing; some of it goes to the church. They was talk once of dressing the rabbits and smaller animals to send back East for city folks to buy and eat, but nobody could figure out how to get them there fast enough. So mostly, the bodies just rot, what the dogs don't tear up and gorge theirselves on.

"Sometimes the men will come back later with guns, to take pot shots at the buzzards circling around overhead for days afterwards. But directly after the kill, the men all head back to the church where the women are waiting for them with hot bowls of vegetable soup or chili, and fresh baked pies. Oh, it's a real celebration, Paramecia! Sometimes I wonder why I even bother with the human race. They is so hellbent on their own destructiveness!"

"But why—" I blurted out, "why do you understand how wrong all this is, when everyone else seems totally ignorant about the consequences of such behavior?"

"I been around longer than most folks, Paramecia," Granny answered. "I come from a different place. I've walked this earth longer than people would guess, and it still don't seem like home to me."

Her voice trailed off softly with these last words, as a strange, wistful look came into her eyes. Then she began humming softly to herself. Finally the words of the song burst from her lips:

"This world is not my own, O Lord,
   I'm just a passing through.
If heaven is not my home, then Lord,
   What will I do?
I'm waiting for a chance to pass
   Through heaven's open doors,
'Cause I can't feel at home
   In this world any more."

It was a strangely sad lament for Granny. She had always seemed so determined and strong, until that moment. I wanted to say something comforting, but at the same time, I did not want to intrude into what were obviously her own private thoughts.

Then it struck me. I was a stranger here myself —out of time, out of place. I wanted to cry out like a little girl, "Father, come get me, please! I want to go home!"

Blindly, I started running up the road, not knowing or caring where I was going, as tears made cold, wet streaks down my face.

"There you are," Shandy said, when he found me down by the creek. "I wanted to go after you right away, but Granny said to leave you be."

"So then, how did you know where I was?" I asked.

"I didn't. But Granny knowed. She always knows. What made you run away like that?"

"I just needed to do some thinking by myself," I answered coolly. I have learned not to express my feelings openly to others. The Collegium does provide group sharing experiences for students. However, attendance is not compulsory so I have never been to one of those things. But I realized it was not fair to let Shandy stand there looking so puzzled and hurt. I had to tell him more than that. What could I say?

Before I found the right words, Shandy, without even knowing anything about my true situation, went straight to the heart of my problem. "You worrying about your pa not finding you yet, ain't you?" he said softly.

I nodded silently.

"Shucks, this place ain't that hard to find," he said. "It's a far walk into town, but I suppose it's time we went in and had us a talk with the sheriff."

"No!" I cried out, jumping to my feet. At that point I made a decision. No matter what lies I had to tell, what stories had to be invented, I would never tell Shandy, or anyone else here, the truth.

How could I expect them to understand? These simple, ignorant people would think I was crazy. What could they know of time warps, of life in the world of 2040 A.D.? No, however sympathetic Shandy might feel toward me now, not even he could understand that.

Except maybe—Granny! Then I realized the absurdity of the sudden thought that had popped into my head. How could I expect Granny to understand, any more than anyone else?

I had to invent something to tell Shandy. "My father is a very clever man," I said. "He—he will find me when the time comes. There are reasons—secret reasons, important reasons—why he can't come for me now." I tried to make the words sound mysterious as possible.

Apparently it worked. Shandy's eyes grew wide with the unexpected possibility of those words. He spoke in a whisper, "Is your pa a bank robber?"

For a second, the strange term puzzled me. I had heard of computer robberies, and occasionally one heard of outbreaks of lawlessness along the conveyor systems. That's why all of us at the Collegium are trained in pressure-point manual defense. We can immobilize an attacker instantly if necessary— but this was obviously not related to any type of random muggings.

"Bank robber?" I repeated Shandy's words, taking my cue from the look of wonder in his eyes. "I can't answer that. Do you expect me to tell you anything that might endanger my father's life?"

Shandy shook his head, his eyes growing larger all the time. "Don't you worry none! You can stay with me and Granny as long as need be—forever, if you have to!"

Those innocent words hit me like a sudden, sharp pain. I turned away, unable to go further with this charade I had been playing. But it is not my fault! I thought bitterly. I didn't know how or why this had happened to me, but I had to go on somehow.

Squaring my shoulders, I turned back to Shandy. "We must go back," I said. "Granny will be worried about us."

When we were almost in sight of Shandy's home,

he stopped and pointed off to the side of the road. "Look there!" he called.

I expected to see some strange new form of wild life, and I looked in the direction of the tall clump of grasses to which he was pointing. At first I saw nothing, then I could make out an animal crouching and trembling in the middle of those dried grasses. It was that half-grown pup of Jake Murty's. As we walked up to it, the dog whined and cringed, then rolled over onto his back in a submissive position, as if to ask our protection.

Shandy bent down and stroked it gently. "There now, nobody's going to hurt you, feller." He kept on soothing and stroking until the animal ceased its trembling. When Shandy rose as if he was planning to leave, the dog whined and came up on all fours. It eyed us so mournfully that Shandy laughed. He scooped up the awkward pup and started walking up the road. It looked so comical dangling there, the head and flapping ears sticking out to one side, the bony tail and hind feet hanging out at the other, that I wanted to laugh myself for the first time that day.

"Well, I guess I got me another critter to look after," Shandy said. "Wonder what Granny'll think of this one?"

The next few days passed slowly and uneventfully, except for the inner turmoil of my thoughts. There were various jobs to perform, and Granny seemed more than willing to let me do my share.

Perhaps she realized my need to get my mind off my troubles, even though I never told her what was bothering me. I seemed to need that close contact with the earth, touching the dirt, watching things grow. I had had so little contact with the natural world of which I was, still, a part. I needed the companionship of working with Shandy and Granny, too. It helped me to feel less like a stranger in an alien land. I even derived a strange comfort from the monotonous sameness of those days.

One of the chores I had to help with was canning the beans from Granny's garden. Shandy hated picking and stemming those beans, but it was a job I rather enjoyed. I had never seen a garden growing in earth—only vast stacked rows of hydroponic tables efficiently growing vegetables in nutrient solutions.

Oddly, the small wild creatures that made themselves at home along the garden rows did not seem to worry Granny. She shooed them off with authority, sometimes imitating animal cries to frighten them away. But after the first early tender things were harvested she let the creatures return to gorge themselves on what was left of the crop. "Ain't no sense in canning more than what we'll use," she explained. "I figure rabbit droppings will make good fertilizer when it's plowed under this fall."

She never ceased to amaze me, that old woman. Her philosophy of acceptance and accommodation to the world around her was truly uncanny. Only humans like Jake Murty seemed capable of arousing her anger. Oh, she pretended to Shandy that she was displeased when he brought that dog of Jake's into the house. But it was only an act. Shandy knew it, and so did I.

The dog *was* a nuisance. In my city, there were almost no household pets. The official policy prohibited large animals, and those those were permitted were under the strictest regulation. No females were allowed to reproduce without special clearance. Any dog caught fouling the conveyor systems with excrement was immediately eliminated. So you see, I found myself agreeing completely with Granny when she grumbled, "That dog ain't going to be nothing but trouble, Shandy. Ain't you had enough orphans to care for around here? Fox kits, birds with broken wings, baby cottontails. Besides, that hound is the biggest coward I ever did see!"

She was right. One moment the dog would be gamboling about, then a sudden noise—a dropped pot, a slammed door—and he would dive for cover beneath the nearest bed. When all was quiet again, he would inch his way out from under the quilts. First, a shiny black nose; then one sad, soulful eye; finally the whole head, those oversized ears of his spread out on the floor like limp pieces of velvet. Granny would frown, put her hand on her hips and shake her head as she said, "Worthless hound!" Then I would see her surreptitiously bending down to scratch behind the pup's ears, and hear the rhythmic thump of his tail on the floorboards.

"Rooster" was the name Shandy decided upon for this new pet of his. The name stemmed from the fact that the first time the dog had ventured into the hen yard he was driven under the bed again, yipping and yelping for help, by Granny's old banty rooster.

I myself had other things to occupy my mind besides the antics of Rooster. I tried to avoid mention of my father in front of Shandy, but he seemed obsessed with this notion of his that Father was some kind of criminal. "I reckon I know," he said confidentially to me one time. "Your pa is one of the Browder gang. He's holed up someplace, and can't get out till it's safe!"

I didn't answer, but somehow that seemed answer enough for Shandy, and he went on spinning out fantasies about my notorious father. I deeply regretted the way I had deceived Shandy. As is often the case, a small lie seemed to grow into a bigger one. However, there was nothing I could do about that now.

Surprisingly, Granny proved helpful in this matter, with that natural, intuitive wisdom of hers. One day I happened to overhear a conversation between her and Shandy. It went something like this: "I wonder when Para's pa is coming for her," Shandy said. "You don't reckon he's got hisself put in jail, do you?"

"Shandy, you just quit pestering Para about that, you hear me?" Granny answered. "I figure she's got

90

enough worries without listening to your foolishness. You just pieced that together out of your own mind, anyways."

"But what if he is a bank robber, Granny? Wouldn't that beat all?"

"The way you take on, Shandy, you'd think bank robbers was some kind of heroes. But they is nothing grand about stealing and killing!"

"I never said there was," Shandy answered. He sounded both ashamed and embarrassed as he said the words.

"I will say one thing, though," Granny added. "It don't make much difference whether stealing and killing is done by bank robbers, or by ignorant folks that steal from the land without putting anything back into it. If you kill off all that's pleasing and beautiful just because it don't seem to be useful, that's a kind of crime too, I reckon."

Apparently Granny's words about my father had some effect on Shandy, because he stopped talking about Father's failure to come after me. As for Granny, it was as if we had some kind of silent agreement between us. I caught her eyeing me once as I was wiping away secret tears, though I turned my head quickly to avoid her penetrating gaze. But I knew she would never speak of my trouble unless I mentioned it first, and of course I never did.

One day after the beans were all picked, canned, and lined up in rows down in the storm cellar, I decided to take Rooster out for a run. I needed some time alone to myself, and Rooster was as good an excuse as any.

The dog loped on ahead, his oversized paws making him look more awkward than ever. He was soon out of sight, but not out of hearing, for I heard his bark from somewhere up ahead. The barking grew louder as I approached, but was oddly muffled as if it came from a tunnel.

I determined Rooster was in some kind of drainage pipe that I saw directly in front of me, running under the road. I peered into the dark insides of that pipe and somehow coaxed Rooster out again. As I grabbed his forepaws to pull him out, I heard a noise beside me.

I spun around, and there, gleaming in the sunlight, was Dingus Murty, wearing my aluminized jumpsuit and my boots! The clothing was too large for him. He had taken up the slack around the waist with some kind of cord, but otherwise the suit seemed intact. I stared at him as I released my hold on Rooster.

"What are you doing with my dog?" Dingus yelled.

"What are you doing with my jumpsuit?" I demanded, my tones matching his in volume. "Give it back to me at once! You had no right to steal it." Somehow, I was obsessed with the notion that if only I could get back into my own clothes, I would also be able to get back into my own world.

I rushed toward Dingus, but he dodged out of my way behind some kind of shrub. My hand brushed against sharp thorns and I drew back, wincing at the sudden pain.

Dingus laughed, which infuriated me. Then he taunted, "They ain't no way you'll ever get this suit back! I'll tear it up first—I swear I will!" And he grabbed at the front of the suit as if to rip it apart if I made another move toward him.

Baffled, I stared at him. "But what do you want with it?" I asked.

"I ain't never seen nothing like this in my whole life," Dingus answered. "I knowed you was rich when I saw it. They's no number of box tops or coupons that would buy a Buck Rogers suit like this one. What would a girl want with such a thing, anyways? It's the grandest, most beautifulest thing I ever saw. Must of cost maybe a hundred dollars. You just keep that worthless old hound if you want to—but you'll never get your suit back. Never!"

He bent down then, and before I realized what he was planning to do, he picked up a rock and hurled it directly at Rooster's side. The instant the rock struck him, Rooster yelped in pain and shot away from me—out of the ditch, over the road, and on into the next pasture.

I have no explanation for what happened to me then, but at that moment I was furious—beyond all reason, beyond all control. I lunged instinctively at Dingus's feet and brought him down in a flurry of dust. I pinched, I scratched, I pulled hair. I dug my nails into that suit and literally tried to tear it off him, all the while screaming words I had not even known I was capable of using. "Dung rat from the sanitation heaps! Sludge worm! Garbage bag!" I screamed.

It was a shameful performance. It still mortifies me to think of it. When the wave of my anger passed, I found myself straddling Dingus, pummeling his chest with my fists. Only then did I realize how unnecessary this had been. If I had really wanted that suit, why had I not simply immobilized Dingus through a vital pressure point? It would have been simple to slip the suit off of him then. So much for reason when passion takes control, I thought.

"Leave off!" Dingus was screaming in my ear. "You can have the suit! I never saw no girl act like that! I'll tell my pa! What kind of she-devil are you, anyways?"

At the return of my sanity, I found I was able to counter his question with one of my own. "And what would you tell Jake we were fighting about?" I asked slyly.

"Oh, he don't care none about that dog," Dingus answered, evading the whole meaning of my question. "It was *my* dog, anyways, till Pa run him off that day."

"Jake doesn't care about the dog; we both know that. But what about stealing?" I was so sure I had Dingus trapped in the web of his own deviousness I released my hold, then stood above him as I stared down. "If your father knew you were a thief, what about that?"

Before I even knew what was happening—as slippery as a snake—Dingus twisted through my legs! He leaped to his feet and took off like a silver streak.

I pursued, but had no better luck catching him than Shandy had had the day before. Finally Dingus disappeared from sight entirely. Despairing, I turned back toward Granny's. I had behaved no better than Dingus himself, and I knew it. He had even outsmarted me. How was I ever going to get back to my own world if I continued to act like some kind of uncivilized primitive from the year 1934?

Why had my emotions become so uncontrolled lately? I needed to review my adaptability training—that was obvious. Perhaps it had something to do with puberty. I remembered Father's words: "Paramecia, you're a sensible girl. The beginnings of adolescence can be turbulent at times, but there is great potential in you. . . ."

The memory stung me with a renewed pain, a fierce longing I could not control, mixed with shame. I had a right to be upset—who would not have been nearly frantic with worry in my place?—but I had lost control when I most needed to keep my wits about me.

There was something else, too, ticking away like a time bomb in my unconscious—something to do with the date and the year, 1934. I had no idea what it was.

9

Coming over a slight rise from the flat expanse of fields and pastures, I saw Granny's house sitting under her carefully watered and tended cottonwood. The tree, like a lacy green umbrella, blocked out the sun's merciless heat and gave color and beauty to the drabness of the landscape. I ran toward the shade gratefully. It was not my home, yet it seemed more like home to me than Room 568 in the Collegium domicile.

As I stepped onto the porch, I heard Shandy's voice from inside saying, "Granny, isn't there no way we can stop the killing?"

Shandy's words stopped me at the door, and I

listened as he went on, "Maybe if folks had my nightmares, they'd stop it. Granny, it's terrible! It's the same dream every time—no plants, no animals— nothing but bare dusty ground everywhere. It's like the end of the world to me, Granny. It's not my world, not any more!"

"Hush, Shandy!" Granny answered. "Don't get so riled up! I swear you act like you been eating magic mushrooms!"

"That's it, Granny!" Shandy cried. "If you could just slip a little something like that into one of them big pots of chili Mrs. Drucker always fixes for the church supper, maybe folks would change!"

"Listen, Shandy!" Granny answered sharply. "We can protect our own, but we can't make other folks do what we want. What's the matter? Them dreams haven't been coming back on you, have they?"

"No."

"Maybe you ought to move back into the house just the same."

"Oh, no, Gran! I've got so I like it out there in the barn. It's just— I got to stop that varmint kill, somehow! I can't hardly bear to think of it."

"I know, it's bad. But Shandy, there's no law that says we got to stay here in Kansas. I could sell this place—maybe get a pretty good bit of money for it. We could move on someplace else; California maybe. I heard tell of places there that hasn't hardly been touched by hunters, or farmers, or lumber-jacks, even. With trees that reach plumb up to the clouds, higher than any old Ozark pine—"

Suddenly the implications of Granny's words hit me like a splash of cold water. I jerked the screen door open. "No! You can't leave!" I shouted as Shandy turned around, startled. "We have to stay here. Otherwise, how will my father find me? Or were you planning to go without me?" I added bitterly.

"Now, hold on to your overhauls," Granny answered. "We wasn't thinking of leaving right this minute, Para. What's troubling you? You look like you been in some kind of cat fight."

"Where's Rooster?" Shandy cut in. "Didn't you take him with you when you went out?"

I had forgotten all about Rooster! My face must have mirrored my dismay, because Shandy went on, "What happened to him, Para?"

"I—Dingus, he—he hit him with a rock and he ran off," I stammered. "Shandy, don't look at me that way! Rooster wasn't badly hurt, but you know what a coward he is!"

"Which way was Rooster headed when you seen him last?" Shandy demanded. Without waiting for my answer, he hit the door frame with his open palm, then rushed on through. "Quick, Para! Was he headed off thataway?"

Shandy pointed off toward the north, and I nodded dumbly. "Then we got to hurry!" Shandy said. "There's no telling what might happen if—"

"If what?" I cried. "Shandy, he's probably hiding under the porch right now. Why are you so upset?"

"It's the varmint kill, Para! If Rooster ran off the

way you said— Well, we just got to go see if we can stop him, that's all!"

Again I found it impossible to keep up. When I was nearly ready to drop from exhaustion I saw what I at first had judged to be a herd of animals in the distance. Shandy was heading straight toward that dark mass, and as I drew closer I heard sounds stranger than any animal sounds. The roar of a crowd inside a stadium, that was what it was like. Yet it was more piercing, more hysterical than that— punctuated by thudding thumps, an occasional sharp crack, and underneath the faint sound of something like whimpering.

I didn't want to go any farther. I had seen enough killing of animals since I had come here. But if Shandy was there—what was worse, if he thought Rooster might be there because of my carelessness— then I had to go on.

By the time I was close enough to make out definite human voices, Shandy was standing at the edge of the long row of men and boys, yelling, "Stop! You got to stop! My dog could be in there with them other critters! I won't let you kill him too. I won't!"

"Get on out of here, Shandy Twigg!" Jake answered. "There's killing to be done. If you ain't got the stomach for it, then go and hide behind your granny's skirts!"

"I ain't leaving!" Shandy yelled back. Then he pointed: "Rooster! There he is! I see him!"

Shandy plunged forward through the rows of men,

and at that same instant I saw Rooster cowering by the wire fence, trembling violently. There were many other animals, too, lunging at the barrier of wire, and falling back. Then there was nothing but confusion. I could see Shandy struggling to get to Rooster.

"He's ruining everything!" Jake roared, rushing toward Shandy. "Get on with the killing, boys! Don't stop now!"

But the men seemed confused by Shandy's presence, and stood haplessly holding their clubs while the animals milled around them.

"It's that damned hound pup!" Jake screamed. "He ain't worth nothing anyway! I'll smash him to a pulp, I will!"

Somehow, I do not know how it happened, Shandy managed to get between Jake and Rooster just as Jake's club swung! I heard the crack—and saw Shandy fall.

"*No!*" I screamed involuntarily, pushing the knuckles of my clenched fist against my teeth.

I could almost hear Granny's words in my ears: "He's too tenderhearted, that boy. It'll kill him one of these days, I reckon." I rushed forward through the crowd of men to get to Shandy, anger surging through me.

When I got to Shandy I stopped. I reached down to touch him, lying there so still and pale. Then I realized he was beyond my help. Instead of grief, however, I felt nothing but rage. Jake was not human—he was a destructive animal!

That rage inside me so clouded my thinking, I had only a hazy awareness of what was happening around me. Granny was there; I knew that much. I saw her standing behind that long wire fence. I remember her lifting her hands to the sky and commanding: "Great Powers of Nature, help me! Dust of the Earth, choke them! Choke them all!"

Then she pointed off in the southwestern sky, and continued, "See! It's coming now! Look there!" As if following instinctive reflex, the men and boys, even Jake Murty, turned to look. They stood silent as roiling black clouds gathered on the horizon.

I was sure Granny's words were pure hocus-pocus, aided by the sudden appearance of those threatening black clouds, but I welcomed that trick of Granny's. It gave me the chance I was waiting for.

Jake Murty stood beside me, holding the bloody club in his hands. I was so close I could see the muscles and tendons working in his neck. This time I would make use of my training in pressure-point self defense. Revenge demanded it, and I was its instrument.

My hand shot out swiftly to touch, then press harder and harder against that spot at the top of the spine. Jake suspected nothing. He gave me one bewildered look, and crumpled under the pressure of my fingers. I had used the technique before in practice sessions. The loss of consciousness was harmless—so long as the pressure was released immediately.

I should have let my hand slip away then. Instead, my arm followed Jake's body as it fell. I watched the breathing grow shallow, almost sensing the slowing of the heart as paralysis deepened. Then, my mind rebelled! What was I doing? At that same instant, I heard a sharp command inside my head: *"Para, stop!"* That was all—one swift, clear message and my fury was gone, drained away like the blood from Jake's face.

I felt my legs beginning to tremble until I thought I would fall over. I had almost killed a man! Another minute, and it would have been too late. No one knew. The others standing there were too confused even to know what had happened. No one knew, that is, but Granny. She eyed me silently, and as our eyes met I knew, I knew absolutely, who had sent me that silent message.

I barely had time to collect my senses when I saw the crowd of women moving toward us. One of the boys—it was Dingus—called out, "Ma! What're you doing here?"

"We heard the news on the radio about—" Mrs. Murty began, then broke off. "What's going on here? Jake!" she screamed. "What's happened to your pa?"

As if in response to her outcry, Jake stirred and sat up from the crumpled position in which I had left him. "What in—? What's going on here?" He shook his head groggily, then stood up.

"Jake, you all right?" Mrs. Murty asked. She

rushed toward him, then stopped as if embarrassed.

"Course I'm all right, woman!" Jake blustered. "But what happened to all the varmints? They was here a minute ago."

I glanced along the wire fence and saw that it was true. Somehow, most of the animals—the ones still alive, that is—had taken advantage of the confusion and vanished.

Then Mrs. Murty looked down at Shandy's still form lying beside Jake's feet. "Oh, the poor thing!" she cried. "He ain't got hisself killed, has he?" I felt the agony of that question, for I was asking it myself.

Mrs. Murty bent down toward Shandy and the crowd pressed closer to watch.

"Don't nobody touch that boy! I take care of my own, I do!" Granny's voice cut through the silence as she pushed down on the wire fence and stepped over it. "Just don't touch him! Get back out of the way! You done enough hurt already."

With more strength than I would have imagined possible in one so old and bent, Granny lifted Shandy in her arms.

"Don't you want us to send for Doc Carter?" Mrs. Murty said, an expression of real anguish in her face. "The boy looks to be hurt bad, Granny. Doc ought to have a look just to see he ain't got one of them concussions."

"I can do for Shandy myself," Granny answered. "He'll be all right, you'll see."

The way she said it, with such certainty, I felt

reassured. Shandy *would* be all right. He had to be! Then Granny added these words: "You best take care of your own selves now, on account of that dust storm coming. It's the worst one ever!"

"What you talking about, old woman?" Jake asked.

"It's true!" one of the women said. "We heard it on the radio. We all better head for cover before it's too late!"

Dust storm! Suddenly bells went off in my head. I knew that date! Was it from something I had seen in the Archival Museum, or something from one of Father's books? About a time when dust storms starting in Texas on May tenth had swept across the country until finally, May 12, 1934, clouds of dust had darkened the skies even in Eastern cities. An insignificant date to some people but not to an ecologist like my father, for that storm had touched off the first large-scale efforts at soil conservation in the world.

But how had Granny known? There was no radio in her house, nothing to give her advance warning. Yet she had known about it. Before it happened, she knew!

As the crowd scattered to their separate homes, I happened to look down. Nestled on the ground, beside a tuft of grass, were two small creatures, babies, abandoned by their mothers or orphaned by the killing. One appeared to be a coyote pup with sharply pointed ears, and cuddled next to him was a tiny rabbit. I scooped them up in my arms, thinking of Shandy and his love for wild things, and turned to leave.

"Hold up a second!" hissed a voice beside me. Dingus sidled up to me then, his eyes darting furtively about as if to make sure no one had seen him. "I got something of yours. You know what!" he whispered. "You just meet me down by the creek soon as the storm blows over. You best be there if you want to get it back! Shhh!" He held his finger to his lips, then darted away.

I shook my head. I wanted no more to do with Dingus or his father ever again. Then I began running to catch up with Granny.

When I caught sight of her carrying Shandy, Rooster was trailing them too. He loped along, sniffing at Shandy's limply dangling foot. As I chased after them, I found myself wondering at the strangeness of all that had taken place.

We didn't make it all the way home before the first strong gusts of wind hit us. Suddenly we were engulfed in swirling dust. Choking, I covered my mouth and nose with the palm of my hand and kept on running.

"This way, Para!" Granny commanded. I made out her form standing at the open door of the storm cellar before she disappeared down the steps. I tumbled after her, slamming the door over us as I came down into the darkness, choking and coughing but breathing in the relatively fresh air gratefully.

A short time later, sitting in the yellowish glow

of that same electric torch Shandy had used to show me the rabbits that first day, I had an odd feeling of closeness and warmth. It was crowded in that cellar. No wonder! There was scarcely room for three people, not to mention Granny's stored provender, a half-grown hound, an orphaned coyote pup, and one baby rabbit. It certainly wasn't roomy, but it was safe.

"Here, Para," Granny commanded, handing me the electric torch. "Hold the light for me so's I can see better."

She had placed Shandy on the cellar floor and was bending over him, one of her hands supporting his head. With the other gnarled hand she parted Shandy's matted hair. For the first time I saw the wound. It was bad! I had no experience with such injuries, but I could tell that much. I turned away, momentarily sickened.

When I looked again—the scalp was whole! Granny was wiping away the last traces of blood with a clean rag. I felt something very close to dread then as I cried out, "What—? How—?"

"Hush, Para!" Granny commanded. "Shandy's coming around now."

Yes, there was no question about it. Shandy's color had returned and his breathing appeared normal. Then he opened his eyes and smiled up at us. "Granny, is Rooster all right?"

"Course he is. And so are you, but I'm giving you some of my strong medicine so's you'll rest good now, Shandy."

Granny pulled a dark bottle from the shelf above her head, uncorked it, and touched it to Shandy's lips. He gulped down a couple of swallows before Granny pulled the bottle away. "That's enough, Shandy. I know it won't kill you, but we don't want no more of them nightmares, neither."

"Para," Shandy said dreamily, "it's the funniest feeling I ever had. 'Most like being drunk, I guess. But it comes to me, there's something I wanted to say to you. I don't know what, exactly." He looked at me surprised, almost as though he saw me for the first time. Then he closed his eyes again, nodded his head, and slept.

"What *is* that medicine?" I said. "And how did you heal Shandy's wound like that?"

All my education had told me that magic was nothing more than superstitious nonsense. I know there are theories about skills of the mind that defy normal explanation, but computers and roboteachers do not deal in such speculative theories. Still, I could not deny the evidence of my own senses. Granny possessed paranormal ability! I had no doubt about that now.

"You *are* a witch!" I exclaimed. "I mean, you really can do impossible things, not just tricks that fool people!"

I half expected her to cackle at my foolishness. Instead, she looked squarely into my eyes and answered, "There is times when folks call me a witch. That's why I can't stay too long in one place. You're always saying how I'm different from other folks.

Well, it's true, Para, I am. I didn't come from this world, you see."

She paused, and the full meaning of her words sank in. She is from another planet—an extraterrestrial! I thought. It had to be. The longing look whenever Granny sang that song about this world not being her home . . . all those other little remarks that seemed to hide a deeper meaning . . . the wisdom she possessed without any formal education at all—and finally, this act of healing! "You—you aren't—?" I stammered.

Granny nodded, but said nothing.

"But how did you get here?" I cried. "I mean, you did say you came from the Ozark hills, and that your people were all gone. Or was that just a fabrication you made up to protect yourself?"

"I did have my own folks once, Paramecia," Granny answered. "We stayed hidden back in the hills as much as possible. I don't live in the past, though, Para. I live in the here and now."

"But your people," I persisted. "Where—where did they really come from?"

"Beyond the stars, that's all they'd ever say," Granny answered. "I don't know what that place was like. But it couldn't of been so much different from Earth or I couldn't of gone on living here all these years."

"How much do you know about me, Granny? I mean, do you know where I come from?"

Granny nodded. "I didn't at first. I thought maybe you was like me, but that didn't fit somehow. Then when you told about that Eco-War, well, it put the last pieces in the puzzle you might say."

"Did you cause that dust storm, Granny? Or did you just know it was coming?"

There was the tiniest quirk of a smile at the corners of Granny's mouth as she answered, "You know me better'n that by now, Para. Figure it out yourself."

"But—how different are you from us?" I cried out thoughtlessly.

Granny laughed. "I ain't got no secret hidden parts, nor nothing like that, Para. You remember that first day you come here, you talked about evolution. Well, I lean to the idea that all of us in the universe comes from some common seed. That's why to me we're all part of one family."

"Yes, I have received training in universal concepts," I interrupted. "I understand that, but—"

"Evolution is a terrible slow thing, Para. Oh, it happens all right. Folks does change. But they don't always get better. Sometimes they goes downhill awful fast. They could even wipe theirselves out if they ain't careful."

I saw what she meant. For all the years of change between Shandy's world and mine, I was no wiser than he, and certainly no better. However, I did have an advantage now in my own world—if I could get back, that is. I had a new understanding of the way all life is bound up together on this earth: a commitment I had not had before.

"Granny," I said quietly, "I'm ready now to re-

110

turn to my own world. I don't know what powers you have, but I place myself in your hands."

She stared at me blankly for a moment. "What are you saying, Para?"

I wanted to shake her for being so cruel! "You have told me who you are. I've seen what you can do. You *are* different—so, help me!"

Granny shook her head slowly. "Para, I can't help you. I didn't have nothing to do with you coming here."

"What do you mean, there's nothing you can do?" I shouted.

"Para, just quiet down and listen!" Granny commanded. "You talk like I be some kind of magic hoodooer. That ain't the way it is at all! I don't even know all the ways I might be different from other folks. That wasn't important, you see. What mattered was finding ways I was the same. One of the ways was in the things I could find to love—the land, the critters, other folks. Oh, it wasn't always easy! Jake Murty it takes some doing just to even tolerate. But Shandy—" here she broke off and her eyes softened—"Shandy was the warmest, tenderest thing I ever held in my arms."

I found my eyes blurring with tears then, but I could not give way to sentiment. I had to know the truth. "And do you know how—I mean, do you have any idea how *I* got here?"

Granny was silent, but I stood there holding her gaze with my own, willing her to reply.

Finally she shook her head. "I been thinking on

that a long while. It wasn't me, Para! I wouldn't of done that even if I'd knowed how. It's best not to play games with other folks' lives. I'm sorry, Para. I don't know what happened."

I accepted what she was saying and stood there on the blade edge of despair. Finally I said, "Well, at least you did try to help me once today, Granny."

"How'd I do that?"

"It was you who sent me that message, wasn't it? When I almost—"

Mercifully, Granny interrupted. "You didn't need me to stop you, Para. You done that yourself. I sent you a message, that's all. Besides, Jake's only human, just like you."

Those words stung, yet I recognized the truth of them. I couldn't call Jake an animal any more. He was no more murderous than I, and at least he hadn't meant to hurt Shandy.

"I have to get back to my own world, Granny!" I cried. "I've already endangered one human life. How long will it be before I become a threat to you and Shandy? Terrible things have happened to me since I came here. I've got to get back!"

Even as I said those words a faint hope stirred in me. Dingus! He had asked me to meet him after the storm was over, to give back my suit. Perhaps I had been right after all. Perhaps getting back into my own clothes would somehow correct the time warp and make the mists reappear. It was the only hope left. I seized it desperately.

My words tumbled out as I explained this to

Granny. "I must hurry!" I said. "Before Dingus decides to change his mind!"

I turned to run up the steps, but Granny stopped me. "He won't be going nowhere and neither will you Para. Leastways not till the dust quits blowing. That'll take a couple more hours for sure."

Then another odd thought struck me. "I seem to remember this dust storm hitting New York and Washington on Saturday, May twelfth. But this is only Friday. How can that be?"

"Dust storms can be terrible things, Para, but they don't move fast like a tornado. By tomorrow this storm'll be blowing dust all over the desk of the President of the United States. Maybe then they'll do something about it."

"But I can't wait any longer!" I cried.

Granny shook her head. "You got all the time there is. Besides, I don't see as you got much choice."

The landscape had altered noticeably by the time Granny would let me leave the cellar. As I made my way toward the spring-fed creek, I saw that a thick covering of dust had turned even Granny's tree into a drooping, gray-green, nightmarish-looking thing. Branches lay scattered beneath it—from the fury of the winds, I supposed. I couldn't walk without stirring up clouds of dust as I moved along. I coughed and then spat up brownish mucus from my throat.

As the sun neared the western horizon, the sky began to turn reddish, then orange, from the filtering effect of the dust particles still remaining in the air. It was eerie. I could almost imagine that I was walking in the desolation of a Martian mining operation. I had never been to the Red Planet, but I had heard it described often enough.

Even the creek area had suffered from the effects of that storm. Some of the water along the edges was brackish-looking and muddy. Where the spring bubbled up, however, it looked so cool and clean it was all I could do not to strip off the overalls I wore and jump in—but I had a more important mission here.

"Dingus," I called, "are you hiding?" I waited for an answer, then tried again. "Come out! This is not the time for stupid games."

I heard a rustling sound then, and Dingus stepped out from behind a dusty willow. He held up my suit. "I changed my mind," he said abruptly, as if anxious to conclude his business with me and then get out. "You can have your suit back," he paused for emphasis, then continued, "if you'll *pay* me for it!"

I felt my hopes fading. "Pay you?" I cried, "How can I pay you? I have no money!"

"Your pa has money, though. You can just *bank* on that!" He grinned at what he obviously considered a very witty remark, and awaited my reply.

"What makes you think my father has money?"

"Everybody's been talking since you been here. Why, Shandy hisself told one of the Drucker kids your pa might be—" he stopped, and lifted one eyebrow while he twisted his mouth knowingly into a sly grin— "well, you know!"

"Whatever Shandy may have said, he knows now that it isn't true," I answered. "What if I should decide to tell your parents about this?"

Dingus shook his head with that infuriating sly look in his eyes. "Oh, no! You ain't going to do that, neither! I seen what you did to Pa today. I don't know *what* you did exactly, but I seen him pass out like he'd been knocked over. Your own pa must of taught you that, I figure. But anyways, I ain't planning to tell, just so long as you pay me for this suit. Then I'll clear out, and you'll never hear nothing from me again."

He waited, while I considered my reply. Should I tell Dingus who I really was? It would terrify him, I knew, if he believed me. He might run away again, to spread who knows what kind of stories about me, and Granny, and even Shandy. He might simply laugh and call me crazy. No, my first resolution to tell none of these people the truth was still valid. I had to find another way.

I settled for a straightforward approach. "You must believe me," I said. "I can't give you anything for the suit. I have no money. What made you change your mind, anyway? I thought you said you would never give the suit back."

I saw the expression on Dingus's face change from slyness to a kind of anguish. "I need the money," he said desperately. "I been saving nickels and dimes every chance I get. I don't kill varmints because I hate 'em! I kill 'em because I get a few pennies for them bounty ears! But now Ma's expecting another baby, and Pa took my money away. I got to get out of this place, somehow, someday! I'd hop a freight train tomorrow, but without some cash, I'd probably starve to death, or end up in jail."

He stopped for a second, while the emotions seemed to build up inside him again. "I hate it here! Pa's always yelling and hitting me! I don't want to be no farmer, nor no varmint killer, neither." He puffed up his chest, as though trying to add inches to his height, as he went on, "I want to *be somebody*—somebody rich—somebody people look at—'stead of dirt poor all my life. And that's why I got to get out!"

I shook my head. Hate, I thought, is nothing but ignorance. Why have I wasted my energy hating Dingus Murty, instead of trying to understand how he came to be the way he is? He is more of a prisoner here in this place than I am. I at least have parents I can remember with pride, and I have Granny and Shandy. What does Dingus have?

"Well," Dingus demanded, "are you going to pay me, or do I rip this thing to pieces right here and now?"

"I understand, Dingus," I said. "Believe me, I do. But I have nothing to give you." Then I remembered something. "Wait! I do have one thing of my own." I fingered the small Möbius band pendant Father had given me. Reluctantly, I released the catch and held it in my open palm toward Dingus.

"This is valuable. It could be exchanged for some coinage. It is solid platinum."

Dingus eyed the pendant suspiciously. "That little bitty thing? I don't reckon I could get more'n a couple of bucks for it!"

In spite of myself, I felt anger stirring in me again. Then I remembered how pitiable Dingus really was, and I said, "At least, let me put the suit on one more time. The pendant *is* valuable, to me at least. Keep it, but let me wear the suit just for a few minutes. I—I need to find out something."

Perhaps it was the earnestness in my voice, but for the first time, I had a sense of full communication with Dingus. He grabbed the pendant. At the same time, he thrust the suit at me. "Take it, then!" he shouted. "But you best not try any tricks, you hear?"

Without bothering to disrobe, I donned my jumpsuit. Then I stood there. I certainly did not feel any different. I looked around. Nothing appeared to have changed. For all its remarkable engineering features of temperature control and heat refraction, that jumpsuit was an article of clothing—nothing more, nothing less. In my desperation I had endowed it with a magical ability somehow to whisk me back to my own world.

What had I expected, exactly? Some sort of molecular transformation, perhaps? I looked down at myself. In that suit I felt more an alien here than ever. I lifted my eyes for one last look in the direction of where that vapor had first appeared.

There! In the dimming light of evening, I saw something! I rushed forward, paying no attention to Dingus shouting, "Hey! Where you going? Come back!"

Then I stopped— It was nothing, only a breath of wind stirring up another small cloud of dust. As the bitterness of disappointment crept around the edges of my mind, I realized I had been as superstitious and credulous in my own way as anybody else.

Slowly, I turned back toward Dingus. I unzipped the suit, tore it from my arms, stepped out of the legs, and tossed it on the ground in front of Dingus. "There, you may have it back now," I said. "It is no good to me."

Dingus stared at me for a moment as if he had been watching some strange rite. Then he grabbed up the suit and darted away.

I sank to the ground, too desolate even for tears. There were no emotions left. No rage, no fear; no longing, even. Nothing but one question: "How can I stay in this place for the rest of my life?"

I don't know how long I sat there. The twilight turned to darkness, and I remember being dimly aware of the moonlight filtering through the branches of cottonwood and willow.

"Para," called a voice softly. It was Granny. She stood above me, though I had not heard her come.

"Have you been standing there long?" I asked.

"It don't matter," she answered. "But I got something to talk over with you."

"It didn't work, Granny!" I cried. "When I put

on the suit, nothing happened. I—I don't know what else to do."

"Listen, Para," Granny said urgently, "I think maybe I do have an answer for you now, if you care to hear it."

I shook my head. "If you're not sure, perhaps you had better wait. I can't bear another disappointment now."

"But there may not be another time, Para," Granny said. "I think—I think maybe it was Shandy that brung you here!"

"Shandy? No—"

"Now wait, Para; hear me out. Maybe Shandy has powers he don't even know about—"

"What are you trying to tell me? Is Shandy—like you?"

"No, Para, that ain't what I mean! You remember that dream he had before you come? And the medicine I give him to cure his bee stings?"

"Was that the same medicine you just gave him a little while ago?"

"Yes, Para—that's what I'm trying to tell you! He commenced to acting restless again, and I thought he was starting to dream—"

"What do Shandy's dreams have to do with me?" I demanded, "Granny, I've had too many false hopes—"

"No, listen. That dream—he kept going on and on about this terrible time when the world would be in danger. Oh, he wanted so bad to help the animals, and there didn't seem to be no way to stop the killing! Don't you see? He wasn't dreaming about now—He must of seen into the future somehow, and called out so strong that you was pulled here to us!"

"You ask me to believe things I cannot understand, Granny," I said. "I know time is a mystery. Einstein made that point over a century ago. Or perhaps he will make it tomorrow—I can't straighten all this out in my mind. But this is too much, Granny! How *could* Shandy be responsible for such a thing?"

"I ain't saying he done it on purpose! Shandy wouldn't of done that. But you don't know how awful that dream was to him—so real, I almost felt like I was there, too!"

"But why me?" I said, still not believing. "It should have been my father, if anyone. He loves the animals much more than I do!"

I paused then, and looked around me. "You must be wrong, Granny. You said you thought Shandy was starting to dream again—but as you see, I am still here."

Granny looked desolate. It was some time before she seemed able to speak again. "I guess I'm just an old fool, Para." Then she held out a box she had been carrying in her arms. "I guess you won't be taking this back with you, neither."

I reached into the box and touched soft, furry bodies.

"It was supposed to be a present," Granny said, "from Shandy's world to yours." Then she shook her head. "Oh, there's so many things about this earth still a mystery to me—why, I don't even know how to die!"

"What do you mean, Granny?"

"Well, Para, I reckon it's just one of the ways I am different. Being born and dying, they ought to go together. But I can't seem to get the hang of it. Maybe if I live to see your world, I could get on one of them space ships and . . . I don't know. Maybe I'll figure it all out someday."

I felt a deep pity then—not just for Granny, but for myself as well. "It is so awful!" I said. "Not being able to get home again! How many years—?"

"Hush!" Granny commanded. "Don't speak of it!"

We stood there in silence, the two of us, lost in a world not of our own choosing. I touched Granny's gnarled hand and knew she understood, for she began singing softly, "This world is not my own, O Lord, I'm just a passing through . . ."

When she finished, I lifted my chin stubbornly and said, "Very well. If this is to be my world now, I will make the best of it. If you and Shandy are to be my family, I will count myself lucky. I will even go with you to California. There is no point in staying here in Kansas any longer."

It was not a joyous decision, but it was a life-affirming one. I got up to go with Granny. There were things to do. There were plans to be made.

"I guess we'd best not forget to take this back with us," Granny said, picking up the small wooden box from the ground.

"Here, let me carry it," I said, taking the box from her. "It was a lovely idea anyway, Granny. Father would have been so—" I stopped, unable to go on.

"No," Granny said brusquely. I looked into her eyes and saw the glint of tears there. Human tears, I thought, as she went on, "It was just a foolish old woman's notion!"

"At least, Shandy will want them," I said. "Granny, is there any chance at all, do you suppose, that my coming here will somehow change things? In the future, I mean?"

Granny shook her head. "The puzzle of time is too much for me to figure out," she said. Then, suddenly, she reached out to touch me, making a strange sound in her throat as she did so.

By the moon's light, I saw an expression of surprise cross her face. She was peering over my shoulder at something behind me. "Look!" she called. "Behind you! That mist!"

I turned around— It looked so different in the moonlight, that waving, almost ethereal cloud of whiteness! Yet it had to be the same. "It *is* the vapor!" I shouted, running toward it. "I can get home again!"

"I *was* right!" Granny said. "Shandy must be dreaming again, Para!"

I halted and turned back. "Granny, come with me!" I begged. "Please! There is a place for you in my time!"

"What about Shandy?"

"He must come too!" I cried.

"Para, think what you're saying," Granny said. "If I wake him up, he'll stop dreaming. Go on, *now!*"

"But we don't know that Shandy—"

"Para, listen! I could go with you; Shandy can't! He ain't growed yet. This is his world, Para, his time. That means I got to stay too. Long as Shandy needs me, that's how long I got to stay!"

124

I stood there for a second, holding the box Granny had given me—then I turned and ran. As I stepped into that ascending, misty curtain, I shouted back: "Good-by, Granny—and tell Shandy good-by, too!"

I don't know whether she heard those words. They may have been lost in the mists of time.

When I started back across the wasteland, things seemed almost—but not quite—as they had been before. I can't explain the transition from night to day, but there are so many things I can't explain.

How can I describe what happened to me? Have you ever been traveling, when you *knew* you were going east, and yet your inner senses told you somehow the direction was west—exactly opposite from the course you intended to travel? Then, suddenly, you saw a landmark—a familiar building, a signpost, whatever—and the whole scene shifted back into its correct perspective. That was how I felt when I saw our ACV still sitting there alongside the deserted highway. My heart sang. I felt such joy I wanted to shout, to lift my hands and cry to the heavens, "I am home! Thank the galaxies, I am home!"

As I ran toward the ACV, I saw Father. He was still talking on the telecom to Mother.

For a second, I felt childish tears welling up in my eyes. I had been through so much; I had discovered so much about myself and the world—and they were still so absorbed with each other, they didn't even know I'd been gone!

Then Father saw me. "Para!" he shouted. "Come here and speak to your mother, will you? She seems to think some terrible thing has happened to you. But it's only been a minute since—" He stopped and stared at me. "What are those clothes you have on? What do you have in that box?"

He pushed me in front of the telecom then, as if to reassure Mother by letting her see that I was really all right. As coherently as possible, I began trying to tell them what had happened. They listened with as few interruptions as possible . . .

Finally, Mother said, "You must stay with us now, Para! I knew it was a mistake to send you away so young. The Collegium can wait."

"What about my studies?" I protested. "Oh, there's so much I need to learn now. I want to know every plant, every bird, every animal—"

"You must give us time to absorb all this, Para," Father said solemnly. "If it is true, and I'm sure that it must be, then how do we know you won't slip away into another time stream—and this time, never come back?"

Suddenly I began to laugh at my foolishness. All this time I had been thinking they were not concerned about me, and here they were behaving like a pair of Granny's broody hens, clucking over one little chick!

"Oh, Father," I said, "stop fretting over me. Just look what's inside the box!" I held up the rabbit then, kicking and squirming with life.

126

Father looked at the rabbit, then at me, an expression of deep thoughtfulness on his face. "Para, did I ever tell you about my great-grandfather? He died long before you were born, of course, but he was once regarded as the leading naturalist of his time."

Naturalist? A short time ago—an infinity ago—I might have answered, "What is a naturalist? Sounds like some kind of freaky cultist to me." But now the unfamiliar word did not bother me. I listened as Father continued speaking.

"He wrote with such passion of his deep love for all living things that he was said to be a fanatic who loved animals more than people. But I think he was right in his beliefs. His name was S. M. Twigg."

"Shandy!" I said softly. "It must have been Shandy . . ."

I still miss Granny and Shandy. I know Shandy is long dead now. Strange to think of him as my great-great-grandfather. As for Granny, perhaps she has broken free at last and found a way to return to her own planet.

Still, whenever I see an aged and stooped figure in a crowd, or standing alone waiting to slip onto a conveyor, I quicken my steps and peer at that aging face, hoping it might be Granny—if she has not wearied finally of her long sojourn with us.

My parents have secured permission for me to join them at their eco-station, in a place that was

127

once a part of the ancient state of Kansas. As I stand holding a new coyote pup, cloned offspring of the one Granny gave me, I remember her words:

"Folks don't never learn, do they? They's always wanting to tame nature so's it'll serve them, and going about it all wrong! Instead of trying to learn how ever' living thing needs ever' other living thing, they just look around and say, 'We don't need that. It don't serve no purpose at all. It's a pest, a varmint. We gotta get rid of it.' But worst of all is when they say, 'I can use that. I can use up ever' bit of it. It's my world! I'll do what I want, and they ain't nobody can stop me!' Sure enough, one day it's all gone, and it's too late to bring things back the way they was before."

The planets and stars are still up there waiting. Someday we may leave this world we have treated so carelessly, venturing out to some new solar system, to a planet as yet untouched and unspoiled. But wherever new life forms are found, we must not subdue and conquer them, only welcome them in their infinite variety, and learn from them. And perhaps—perhaps Granny will be there too, waiting for us.